Once upon a time, everything fell apart.

EVERYWHEN

Savage Princess: Book one

Liberty Freer

Cover Designer: Dark City Designs.
Edited by: My brother's editor.
Proofread by: Moonlight proofreading

Contents

CHAPTER 1

The sheet is ripped away from my body. The air from the fan cools down the exposed skin on my legs and back. Covered in sweat, I'm on my stomach and sprawled across the twin-size bed. God, I hate this bed. Each spring digs into my skin, and every morning I feel like I've been hit by a truck.

"Get up. We're going to be late. You promised me, Hayley."

I groan into my pillow. "Late for what?" I lift my head, brushing unruly hair from my face so I can see my sister. She's wearing the knee-high, soft pink dress she wore to my high school graduation last year. The fact that it still fits her is proof that she isn't going to grow anymore. I should rub it in her face that I was right when I told her she wasn't going to be taller than the five-foot-one that she is, but her angry expression has me biting my tongue.

A white headband keeps her bangs out of her

light blue eyes, and her dark blonde hair is pulled into a high ponytail, the end reaching the middle of her back. Her simple pink dress and petite stature have her looking twelve rather than almost sixteen.

I roll on to my back, and the breeze from the fan cools down my sweaty stomach. "Why are you dressed up?"

Tilly rips the pillow from under my head and tosses it at the foot of the bed. "You forgot? Oh my god, Hayley! You suck! I reminded you last week. Get up. We need to go." Glaring at me, she crosses her arms. "I'm glad I had Margo's mom bring me home early. You have the worst memory."

She's right about that. I'm a scatterbrained mess. Sleep deprivation will do that. I sit up, swinging my legs over the mattress. "Late for what?" I grab my phone from the dresser that's crammed between our beds. "Fuck, it's only eight. I'm working tonight. I had my alarm set for ten." I rub my eyes. I was up until four in the morning, tossing and turning. The new sleeping pills I got from the doctor aren't working, but I wasn't expecting them to. The prescription before this didn't either.

"The interview." She grabs my arm, straining to pull me up because she's so much smaller than me. "You need to get dressed."

Brushing her away, I get to my feet and stretch. "That's still on? I thought they found her?"

Tilly rummages through the dresser drawers

and then throws purple fabric at me. "There was a mix-up. It turned out it wasn't her."

I hold up the ugly ass blouse and then toss it back. "How does that happen?" With the Westlings being such a wealthy family, one would think they'd have the best people working on finding their long-lost daughter. I adjust my sports bra and then bump Tilly out of the way so I can grab my favorite band tee from the floor. I pull it over my head and kick my pajama bottoms off. I wiggle into black skinny jeans that have rips over the tops of my thighs.

Tilly's pink lips pull down. "You can't wear that. Nobody will believe you're Anna Westling if you go looking like that."

I roll my eyes. "You're the one who wants to be Anna." I grab the spare keys from the top of the dresser and shake them. "I'm just the ride."

Tilly huffs. "You promised you'd interview with me, that we'd do this together."

"And I am. That doesn't mean I think I am or even want to be Anna." I groan thinking about the thousands of girls between the ages of fifteen and twenty-one that will be there. It's going to be a fucking madhouse. I slip my feet into my checkered Vans and then throw my hair up into a messy bun. "Gotta brush my teeth."

Tilly crosses her arms and taps her foot. "Hurry up."

"Yes, boss," I mumble even though there's no point in hurrying. If it's anything like the past interviews I've seen on TV, people will have started lining up before the sun. The interviews are legendary. Tilly has been begging to go since the Westlings started hosting them two years ago, but none were close enough to home until now. I guess that's a perk of moving in with our grandma and not going to stay with Aunt Kathy in her much bigger house hundreds of miles away in Texas.

After brushing my teeth, I splash cold water on my face, trying to clear the fog from my brain. I'm going to need some major caffeine. The bathroom door rattles as Tilly bangs on it and yells for me to hurry up. I swing it open and brush past her, but she's right next to my side a second later. "Bring something to keep busy. It's going to be a long-ass wait." She's a talker, and if she doesn't bring something to keep herself entertained, I'll be fucked.

Tilly smirks, leaning against the doorframe while I dig under my bed. "Or we'll get moved to the front of the line because you fit Anna's description to a T, and you actually look like Aiden. You could totally be his missing twin."

"I look like a lot of people, Tilly." And it's true. When I was little, I went through a phase of comparing myself to every person with brown hair and blue eyes. Like most adopted kids, we have aunts, uncles, cousins, and half-siblings out in the world that we have never met.

"If we get moved to the front of the line, I'll give you my leather jacket." I laugh because there is no way that's happening. I find the small fireproof safe I was looking for and set it on the bed.

Tilly grins, and I almost feel like giving her my jacket. She's been smiling so much less since Mom died.

"You're on," she says. "Now for real, hurry up." She rolls her eyes and walks away.

So impatient. I guess it is every little orphaned girl's dream to find out you're royalty, and in this case, literally. Anna Westling's mother, Nora Westling, is a princess of Sweden... No, Switzerland, or was it Finland? Wherever she's from, Anna Westling was kidnapped from her American home at the age of three, leaving behind her mother, father, and two brothers, one her twin. I think the Westlings had another kid a few years ago. There hadn't been much about them in the news until the interviews. Maybe they started holding them for publicity. Most everyone thinks Anna is dead.

I grab our adoption papers from the safe, place them in my green crossbody bag, and then head into the living room. Tilly's sitting on the floral couch, and Nana's on the recliner, explaining in every boring detail the proper way to crochet the ugly blanket she's working on.

Tilly looks at me and frowns. "Can you at least change your shirt? They aren't going to believe you're one of them if you don't look like it."

"We aren't trying to convince them, Til." I laugh. "You want me to lie my way in?"

She pops a shoulder.

"Where are you girls going?" Nana asks, not

bothering to look up from her sole purpose in life: her yarn.

"The Westling interview, Nana." Tilly says. "I told you about it the other day."

Nana scratches the back of her head, careful not to bump one of the many pink rollers in her hair. "Westling? That actor? You going to the movies?"

"Something like that, Nana. I'm taking your car." She opens her mouth, but I'm quicker. "I'll have your car back in time for you to go to bingo." I pull Tilly out the door and head for the silver sedan in the driveway. My sister's bright smile will be worth the torture I'm about to endure. Thousands of groupies, here we come.

CHAPTER 2

I've never seen so many brunettes in one spot, but I bet half of them have dyed their hair to fit the part of what Anna Westling would look like. This is my first time at the Chattanooga Convention Center, and I didn't know it would be so big. When I first walked in, it reminded me of an airport with wide-open walkways, signs posted on every wall, and escalators and bathrooms galore.

Tilly and I followed signs that led us to exhibit room D. Apparently, rooms A, B, and C are full. About twenty girls have come in since we got to this room an hour ago, and we waited in a line outside for an hour before getting in. There are at least two hundred girls in this room. There aren't tables or chairs, so some of the girls have dropped down to sit on the floor, including me. Tilly is still standing, eyes scanning the room constantly. I'm tempted to lie back and try to sleep, but the constant chatter of all the girls would probably prevent that.

Tilly tried to make me stand when men walked into the room a few minutes ago, plucking girls from the crowd and directing them out of the room. Either the girls snuck in or they are Anna look-alikes and are moving ahead. We had to show our papers at the door to enter, and we were told we'd have to show them again at the actual interview.

"My ass hurts. They could have set up chairs," I mumble. I never had a chance to get caffeine, so I feel like shit. "I'll give it one more hour, Til."

She ignores me, standing on the tips of her toes trying to see over everyone. I know who she's looking for, who all these girls want to see, Aiden Westling, Nick Cabot, and Casey Brooks. It's kind of sick. They are crushing on Aiden but also want to be his sister. I don't see what the big deal is. Yes, Aiden Westling is attractive and a multi-millionaire, but I've never seen a picture of him smiling. He always looks pissed off.

His best friends, Nick and Casey, are always by his side. They usually look grumpy as fuck too. I'd think they were in some kind of threesome relationship if it wasn't for Casey's on and off again relationship with Morrisa Shay, some pop singer who I don't listen to. Maybe Nick and Aiden are together like the rumors suggest. I've never seen them photographed with any girls.

I elbow Tilly in the shin. She keeps losing her balance and bumping into me. "Quit. Aiden isn't going to slum it in exhibit room D."

The girl in front of me turns her head to glare before lifting her chin and facing away again. She tried talking to me about thirty minutes ago, but I cut that shit off quick. No way am I going to spend my time making pointless conversation with a stranger.

Tilly scoffs. "He's here somewhere. He attends every event." She moves out from the line, raising her hands in the air, and then her piercing scream bounces off the walls, freezing me and everyone in the room. She doesn't stop until I jump up and slap my hand over her mouth.

"What the hell?" I growl. I look around thinking maybe she saw Aiden but the only males in the room are the two meaty security guys.

My skinny little shit sister wiggles out of my hold and skirts to the side, jumping up and down with her arms waving wildly above her. "Anna's over here! Hey!"

Now I see what she's doing. She didn't see Aiden. One of the bodybuilder guys is close and this crazy bitch is trying to get his attention. She must be desperate for my jacket. I hold in my smile. Even though I hate that everyone's staring at us, I'm glad to see my sister's spitfire personality shining through.

The girl in front of me whispers to the girl in front of her, but all I pick up is crazy. They both giggle, and I feel my face heating up. "What'd you say?" I crouch down next to the girl that tried to start a conversation with me earlier. She's my age, or maybe a year younger. "Are you talking shit about my sister?"

Her small face pales. "No." Her voice comes out in a squeak.

I roll my eyes, losing some of my anger. She probably faked her papers or was adopted at a young age. Girls like her don't grow up in the system. She begins to shake, and the girl she was talking to turns her back.

"Yo, you big dummy, over here!" my sister yells, taking my attention off the brat. "I bet you a thousand dollars I have the real Anna!"

"Okay, that's enough." I grab her arm, pulling her back into line.

"A thousand dollars, huh?"

A blond meat head stops next to us, his massive frame creating a shadow over us. His white shirt is stretched so tight over his muscular chest it looks like it might rip in half. He has a few wrinkles around his brown eyes. I'd say he's mid-thirties, but he keeps his body in shape, making him appear younger. His gaze moves from my sister to me, and his amused smile slips away.

With furrowed brows, he takes in my appearance. "Yeah, okay," he says after a beat. "She can move up, but I'll be expecting my money, kid." He chuckles and gestures for us to follow him.

"Told you," my proud sister whispers to me.

Mr. Beefy has made her day because we're ushered away from the line and into an office-like waiting room where several other girls who have features like mine sit. Tilly keeps whispering *oh my god*, over and over as we follow Mr. Beefy through the room of wannabe Anna's and into a smaller room that looks like the interrogation room cops use, but instead of a table, there's a wooden desk. Mr. Beefy takes the chair behind the desk and Tilly and I take the two chairs in front of it.

He stares at the screen of the laptop in front of him. "Are you both interviewing?"

"No, just Hayley."

My gaze snaps to my sister. "What?"

She snorts. "I wanted this for you. I know where my birth mom is. I even have a few baby pictures of myself. It's highly unlikely that I'm Anna Westling but you..." She shrugs. "It's possible."

I laugh. "This is ridiculous. I'm only here because I thought *you* wanted to interview." I get to my feet. "If you're not doing this—" The panic in her eyes freezes me. I hate to see her upset.

"Please, Hayley. Just interview. Please, for me? I'll never ask you for anything else. You're already here."

She looks like she's about to fucking cry. I will never hear the end of it if I walk out now. Letting out a long breath, I drop back down and focus on Mr. Beefy. "Let's get this over with." I hand over my adoption papers.

He shuffles through them and then drops them next to the computer. "I'm going to ask you a few questions. Answer them honestly and to the best of your ability. If I like your answers, you'll move on to the next step." I nod. "What's your earliest memory?" Not paying attention to me, he taps at the computer keys.

I squint. I have a collection of early memories, but the timeline is skewed. I'm not sure which one is the earliest. "Riding a bike," I say.

Tilly's leg stops bouncing. "No, it's not. You didn't learn to ride a bike until you were twelve. I was there, and Dad recorded it."

"Shouldn't you be running a DNA test on me?" I ask Mr. Beefy, ignoring my stupid sister.

"There are thousands of girls here, you want me to test them all today?" He stands, glancing at my sister and then back at me. "You're wasting my time if you're going to lie. You don't even want to be here."

Tilly jumps up, visibly shaking. "God, Hayley! Tell him. One of her earliest memories is being taken away from a foster family," Tilly says in a rush. "She used to have nightmares about it."

I could smack her. That is nobody's business. Pain slices through my chest at the memory of my foster family, but Tilly's wrong, that's not my earliest memory. That memory opens the floodgates to all the other families that didn't want me. Memories that I've worked so hard to bury deep.

Fuck.

Plant in the corner, desk, concrete floor. I begin listing off the things in the room to help myself

17

stay in the present and calm down. Two-way mirror. *Wait, what?* "Are we being watched?"

"No." Mr. Beefy slowly sits back down. "Sometimes but not right now."

Tilly's gaze widens. "Aiden's been back there?"

Her obsession with him is too much. She's willing to out my fucked-up past to meet him. I shoot her a death glare before turning back to the wall of muscle. "Next question."

He sighs. "How many homes were you in before you were adopted?"

I narrow my eyes. "I didn't keep count. If I had to guess, I'd say... twenty."

"Do you remember your birth parents or know who they are?" He types something into the computer. "You'll be twenty in November. Did you look at your records when you turned eighteen?"

I shake my head. "I was told my birth parents were some gang banger drug dealers." I cross my arms.

Mr. Beefy types at the computer, his brows furrowing. "The state never found your parents. You have no biological siblings." He types in something else, and I'm wondering how he found all this information. "No extended family was found either," he mumbles, and then his eyes meet mine.

He's not telling me anything I don't know. I was told the same things. My mom said she was told that I was found bruised and dirty a block from home. I was taken to the police station, and when the cops went back to the house to speak with my parents, there was a shootout, several cops were killed, thousands of dollars' worth of drugs were found, but my parents and a few of their friends escaped. They found my birth certificate and my birth mom's ID.

"You had blonde hair?" Mr. Beefy mumbles, spinning the computer to face me. The earliest picture of me stares back. "This you?"

It's a picture that was printed in the paper when the state of Tennessee tried to find my family members. My hair was platinum blonde and cut into a short bob. "That's me."

He peers at my messy bun. "You dyed your hair brown?"

"This is my natural color. It was blonde when I was little."

"They could have dyed it," Tilly says, leaning forward. "Later pictures of her look like it was dyed by the way the roots came in."

I jerk my head to my sister. I've never heard her say she thought that. "What the hell are you talking about? No lying. I'm not trying to be someone I'm not."

"I'm not lying. I've thought about this, Hayley. I knew how you'd react if I brought it up."

Mr. Beefy nods and turns the computer toward me again. Seven-year-old me fills the screen. My sapphire eyes are watery and pink lips pulled into a frown. The top half of my hair is brown but from the ears to my shoulders, it's blonde. That was taken when I went to stay in a group home.

"She was late losing all her baby teeth. Our mom said it was because she was a late bloomer, but maybe it's because she was a year and a half younger."

"Tilly!" I stare at my sister. "What the fuck?"

"I told you I've thought about this. Anna Westling would have turned eighteen a couple months ago. You struggled academically in school, were the smallest in middle school, and were a late bloomer in everything. Maybe it's because you're younger than your birth certificate says."

I can't tell if she believes what she's saying or she's making this shit up on the fly because she wants to lie my way in.

Getting to his feet, Mr. Beefy points at Tilly. "You, step out the door for a second. I need to talk to Hayley alone."

Tilly is all too eager to listen and jumps to her feet.

"Hold up," I say, catching her wrist before she can walk out the door that Mr. Beefy is holding open. "I'm not leaving my sister alone so you can harvest her organs or some crazy shit like that."

Tilly rolls her eyes and bounces away, happily taking a seat in the chair by the door. "I'll be fine. I'm not a baby."

"Fine," I mumble through a clenched jaw. I focus on the hulking man. "Hurry up."

Once the door's closed, I glare at him. "I'm not taking my clothes off. I've heard rumors about what happens at the interviews."

He plucks a paper and pen from the desk drawer and sets them on top. "Sign this."

I scan the paper, an NDA. It's pretty cut and dry, so I fill in the information and sloppy sign a fake name. "Done. What now?"

Mr. Beefy steps up to me and motions for me to turn around. I give him my back, glancing at the window. "Is someone in there now?"

"No. We're being recorded though."

I feel his fingers at the back of my neck, parting my hair. "Are you checking for lice because I haven't had that since I was like twelve."

"Fuck."

His whispered breath has me on edge. *Fuck? Why fuck?* "You didn't find any, right?" My scalp begins to itch at the thought of those tiny bugs. Lice are the worst. Having to comb through my hair would be a nightmare. I'd end up cutting it short.

His fingers leave the back of my neck. "I'll be damned. I owe the kid some money."

I look over my shoulder. "What'd you see?"

Smiling, he steps back. "What I needed to. It's nice to meet you, Miss Westling. My name is James Gregory, and I've been searching for you for a very long time."

CHAPTER 3

With narrowed eyes, I tilt my head to the side. "Are you fucking with me? Is this part of the test?" I eye at the two-way mirror. "You want to see how I'll react or some shit?"

"I'm sure the news is overwhelming, but you are Anna Westling." He smiles wide, brown eyes shining, probably with humor from his ridiculous joke.

"And you think I'm her because of the back of my neck?"

"There's a mark only a Westling child can have. You'll take a DNA test, but it'll be a match."

I stare at him for a minute, waiting for him to say he's kidding. There is no way in hell he's serious. He doesn't say anything, but his smile slowly falls, and he stares at me like I'm the weirdo. He probably expected me to start screaming with joy or some shit.

When his phone breaks the silence and pulls his

attention away from me, I grab my purse from the chair and snatch my papers from his desk. "I don't like being fucked with." I give the two-way mirror my middle finger. "You're lucky I didn't want to be her. This is sick."

Mr. Beefy looks up from his phone. "What?"

Rolling my eyes, I push past him. Tilly jumps to her feet when she sees me, no doubt seeing my furious expression. Not slowing my pace, I grab her arm and pull her with me.

"Wait!" Mr. Beefy calls after me. "Hayley!"

I pick up the pace, and Tilly grills me with questions. When I don't answer, she tries to slow us down by dragging her feet. All I have to do is shoot her a look and then she's running with me down the main hall toward the double doors that lead to freedom.

I look over my shoulder, expecting Mr. Beefy to be following, but he's not. I only see a long line of girls against the wall on my left. I push open the doors, we speed down the sidewalk, and then move across the street to where I parked Nana's old car. My foot smashes down the gas pedal before Tilly's had a chance to snap her seatbelt into place.

"What the hell?"

I stomp on the break right before turning out of the parking lot and shift the car into park. "The interview was bullshit." I don't understand what just happened or what the point was in lying, and it had to be a lie. I remember my mother and she wasn't Nora Westling.

"What do you mean?"

I twist in my seat, giving Tilly my back. "Do you see something on my neck?"

"Like what?" Tilly brushes her finger over my neck. "There's nothing there."

I scoff, turning back to face the windshield. "Nothing." Mr. Beefy didn't even chase me. If he really thought I was Anna, he wouldn't have let me leave. Unless... chasing me would have caused a scene and he didn't want thousands of girls freaking out.

He said he knew I was Anna because of my neck. Like necks are so diverse they can be used to identify someone. Maybe he wanted to see if I was stupid enough to believe his twisted joke? Maybe the Westlings are trafficking girls. They could be selling the poor girls who believe the lie. I shake my head. I'm not going to analyze this bullshit. If I wanted answers, I shouldn't have run, but thinking logically while my emotions are heightened has never been my strong suit.

"You're not going to tell me what happened?"

I contemplate what telling her would mean. She'd demand we go back, and I'm not doing that. "They wanted me to take my clothes off, and the interview was recorded."

Tilly's face scrunches up. "Gross. Are you serious?"

"Yeah." I pull out of the parking lot, taking the turn sharply.

"Why would the Westlings want the girls to get naked? That's really weird."

"I signed an NDA, so don't tell anyone what I said. I could get sued."

She slumps down in the seat. "Okay. Sorry I talked you into going. I thought you could be her." Her voice sounds small, and she looks so sad as she picks the blue polish on her fingernails.

"No biggie." I smile. "I just wish you would've gotten to see Aiden. Maybe then that shit show would have been worth it."

She stares out the window. "I don't want to see him now. They're a bunch of freaks."

"Right," I say, feeling slightly guilty my lie ruined Aiden's image for her. "Hey, why don't we get pizza and ice cream?"

Tilly eyes me. "You said we didn't have enough money for eating out."

I shrug. "I got some extra shifts coming up. I think we can afford lunch."

A smile breaks free. "If you're sure we can afford it then yes. Yay!"

Pizza and ice cream for the win.

***

Two hours later, I pull up the driveway and pull the keys from the ignition. "I ate too much." I glance at the clock on the dash and deflate. It's already time to get ready for work.

Tilly quickly unbuckles her seatbelt. "I'm going

to pee my pants. I shouldn't have drunk that third soda."

She flies out of the car and races toward the house. I'm slower because I need caffeine. I drudge up the concrete steps to the narrow porch. Nana's house is a small two-bedroom, but it's clean, clutter-free, and there's another adult to help me with Tilly so she can remain a kid.

I kick my shoes off next to my bed and grab my work clothes from the top of the dresser. I text Trent again to see if he's picking me up. I messaged him when we got to the restaurant, and I still haven't heard from him. I pull on black slacks and tuck in my red button-up shirt so it doesn't hang to my knees.

I kick back in bed waiting for my douchebag boyfriend to text me back. We have to be at work in thirty minutes. If he doesn't let me know something soon, I'll fork out the cash to Uber. I've been saving as much money as I can in case I need to start helping my grandmother with the bills. She's paying Dad's mortgage while he's taking time off work. I've offered her money, but she won't take it. She says I need to put it into savings.

"Margo's here." Tilly throws a bunch of crap into her oversized purse.

"Just bowling, right? Do you need a ride home?"

"We might go to the movies after. Brittany and Natalie are going. Brittany's mom is going to bring me home." She ditches her dress for jeans and a teal tank top.

I hold out a couple of twenties. "Call me if you need anything. I get off work at eleven."

She bites her bottom lip, staring at the money, but ultimately takes it. "Thanks, Hayley. Love ya. Bye."

She hurries out of the room as a blaring car horn comes from the front. Tilly yells that Trent's here even though I already knew. My sweet boyfriend lays on the horn again to let me know he's arrived instead of texting me like a normal person. I slip on my checkered Vans and shove my phone into my pocket.

Trent's smoking a cigarette in his beat-up Honda. My stomach sinks. I'm sick of pretending with him. After my mom died, I was in rough shape, and Trent knew where all the parties were. He had a big group of friends and good weed. Plus, he was an easy ride to work. Getting with him was a way to keep my mind off the pain, and now, it's because I'm using him for his car.

He flicks the half-smoked cancer stick out the window when I open the passenger door. "Hey, babe. How's it going?"

I drop down in the seat and shut the door. "Fine."

He looks over his shoulder as he backs the car down the driveway. "When you moving back home? Coming here is way outta the way."

It's not. My nana's house is twenty minutes from home. "I don't know. Probably a few months. I can give you more gas money." I snap my seatbelt into place. I didn't use to wear one, but Mom's accident changed that.

As we ride down the road, he flicks his head to the side every few minutes to get the hair out of his eyes. It's been driving me nuts lately. He has the same hairstyle as a freshman in high school.

"You thought any more about taking Stephanie's spot?"

"Told you before, waitressing isn't for me."

He flicks his head. "Yeah, babe, but it'll be more money. We could get a place."

I don't want to move in with him for multiple reasons. First, no way in hell am I leaving my little sister. Second, I don't like him enough. I'm not even really attracted to him. He's not my type, personality-wise or looks. "Trent, if I took Stephanie's spot, I'd end up in jail from killing a customer. I'm looking at other jobs anyway."

"Damn, Hayley. I'm ready to get out of my mom's house. She's trippin´ all the damn time."

"I know."

He rests his hand on my thigh, inching toward the center. "We have a little time. Wanna stop real quick?"

"I'm on my period," I lie. I had sex with him a couple of times at the beginning of our relationship because I was trying to scratch an itch, but it was never worth it. He pounded into me for a minute, and then bam, done. I don't know why he keeps trying. I heard he hooks up with his ex. I'm going to break up with him soon.

"Damn, again? Weren't you on your period last week?"

"Red light," I say because he's focused on me and not the damn road.

He cusses and hits the brakes. The light turns green the second he stops and we're moving again.

Another couple minutes and we pull into the parking lot at work. As soon as the car stops, I grab my purse and scoot out the car. Daffy's is one of the more popular restaurants in our small town. We walk inside, and I shove my purse under the U-shaped hostess counter. Trent heads to the bathroom, and I head to the break room.

Angie, Ronald, and Carmen are lounging around the small table that seats four. Management removed the second table a few weeks ago thinking people would talk less and work more or some shit. Angie and Ronald are wearing the restaurant's attire: black slacks with a red button-down shirt. Carmen is wearing teal leggings and the ugly orange work shirt that only she can pull off. Her eyeshadow is hot pink and so is the scrunchy that's holding her dark blonde hair into a high pony.

Carmen is the one I talk to the most. Everyone is nice, a little nosy, but nice. I grab my timesheet and push it into the slot that stamps it with the time.

"Hey, girl, hey," Carmen says, grinning. "Did Tilly get to interview today?"

I frown, crossing my arms. "How'd you know

about that?"

Carmen laughs. "Tilly was up here last month beggin´ you to agree to take her."

"Oh yeah," I mumble, leaning against the wall. "I took her. She's not Anna."

"Damn," Carmen says, her pouty lips pulling down. "I was hoping for a ticket outta here."

"Like she'd give you money," Ronald says, grinning but quickly pulls in his smile. He had a tooth pulled last week, but it's only noticeable when he smiles wide.

"Nah, it's a good thing," Angie says, pulling her curly red hair into a bun. "They may be rich as hell, but that family has some serious issues."

"That's true." Carmen's honey-colored eyes narrow. "I don't think the girls interviewing know what they're getting themselves into. You'd be constantly watched and talked about. Nothing would be private anymore." She shakes her head. "Fuck that. I'm not signing away my freedom. None of the kids look happy. Especially Aiden Westling."

"Dude, his twin sister was taken. I think that gives him a reason to look like that," Angie says, and then smiles and wags her brows. "I bet I could put a smile on his face."

Carmen blows a bubble with her gum and then pops it loudly. "No wonder Nora turned to drugs. She's probably depressed. She lost her daughter and her husband is never around." She looks at Angie and rolls her eyes. "And as if. Everyone knows Aiden plays for the other team."

Bane, who reminds me more of a college frat boy than a cook, steps in with his apron in his hands and Trent trailing behind him. "What are you guys talking about?"

"The interview. Hayley took Tilly today."

"Oh yeah? I thought that was Saturday?" Bane says.

Ronald chuckles. "Today is Saturday."

Bane tilts his head to the side, studying my face. "You didn't interview? You could be Anna Westling. Weren't you adopted like Tilly?"

Carmen pops her gum. "You really could, Hayley." She swipes at her phone screen and then gets up to hold it up to me. I study the image. We do look similar, but so did hundreds of other girls at the interview today. "Dude, see. You and Aiden look alike. That's freaky. You have the exact same eyes." She studies the picture. "Nora's eyes are hazel, and John's are brown, so I don't know where Aiden got his eye color."

"Damn, they do look alike," Bane says, leaning over my shoulder to better see the picture on Carmen's phone. "Look at the chin. They have the same chin."

"No way." Trent scoffs and then laughs. "I can't even picture her as a princess or in a dress. She looks nothing like that family." He leans closer to the picture and shakes his head. "Pull up a picture of Nora. Hayley looks nothing like that. Nora's hot as fuck."

Finally, someone with some sense. It's not usually Trent but right now he's the only logical one here.

"Take out her facial piercings, tame the hair, makeup the face and she would fit right in," Bane says. "She could be a hot as fuck princess. Maybe she should pretend to be Anna to get some money."

"I bet the rumors about Nora killing Anna and hiding the body are true," Trent says. "Hot bitches are always crazy as fuck."

"Dude, that's what I've always said," Ronald says, snapping his fingers and pointing at Trent.

"God, you guys are so morbid," Angie says.

"Okay." I squeeze between Bane and Trent, putting myself closer to the open doorway. "I wouldn't want to be a part of that shit show. Like Carmen and Angie said, that family has way too many issues."

"Wait, didn't they find Anna?" Bane asks. "A couple months ago or something."

"I heard that the lab reported the test out wrong," Angie says. "Or they lied. Either way, it wasn't Anna."

I'm nearly out of the room when Lisa's much bigger body almost collides with mine. I shuffle back a few steps and take the spot next to Trent.

Lisa claps her hands loudly three times. "If you're on the clock, get to work. Now, guys. It's getting busy up front."

She's an ex-cop and not someone to take lightly.

She's almost six-foot-tall with a full sleeve on her right arm and a strong jaw that's always tensed. When Lisa says move, you better listen.

The little pow-wow that has my gut-churning, breaks up. I really hope what happened at the interview was a fucked-up hoax, but on the slim chance that Mr. Beefy was being serious... My whole body breaks out in a cold sweat.

"Hayley, wait," Trent calls before I can make it into the dining area. "When it slows, let's get cut first so we can hit up Danny's party."

"Definitely," I say because I'm going to need all the mind-altering substances to put this day behind me. "His parties go late, even if we get off on time, we can still go."

"Rush coming in, Hayley," Lisa says, sounding aggravated.

"Yep, on it." I brush past her and move to the front of the restaurant where Lilly, the other hostess, is impatiently waiting for me so she can go smoke. I escort four separate families to tables and then move to the register to cash people out. The claw machine takes a little girl's money, and she cries so hard that she pukes all over the floor. I clean that up, seat a dozen more families, and then get a couple of to-go orders ready.

When it finally starts to settle down, I lean against the counter and watch the waitresses in the dining area for a bit before doing something I'm not supposed to—play with my phone.

"Miss Westling."

I'm scrolling through social media when the deep voice has goosebumps breaking out all over my body. I don't want to look up, but I do. Mr. Beefy is at the other side of the counter with his arms crossed over his broad chest.

"One?" I ask, grabbing a menu from the top of the stack and hoping he doesn't see the way my hand shakes. I never thought I'd see him again. He let me leave. If he wasn't fucking with me... If he really thinks there's a chance I'm Anna... This is not good. I glance to my left, hoping nobody I work with has noticed him.

He lifts a brow. "I think we both know I'm not here to eat."

I set the menu down. "Guess you're in the wrong place. This is a diner. Have a nice day." I move my focus back to my phone only to have Mr. Beefy snatch it from my hand.

"We can do this the easy way or the hard way. I need to swab the inside of your cheek. You ran off before I could."

I'm fighting myself not to lunge for my property in his hand. "You said you don't DNA test the inter-viewers."

He pockets my phone. "I said we don't test them *all*. We test the ones who we think are Anna. We've only ever tested one."

"What makes you think I'm her?" I ask casually like I don't care, but I do. I need to know why he thinks it, so I can convince him otherwise.

"Your past." His gaze darts to the right and then

moves back to me. He lowers his voice, and says, "And what I saw on your neck." He crosses his arms. "Are you going to cooperate or not?"

"Maybe. Give me my phone." I hold out my hand and glare. "And there's nothing on my neck. My sister checked. What do you think you saw?"

"A mark."

"What kind of mark?"

"Test and then your phone."

I glance to the left again. Angie's helping a table but her gaze cuts to me. The table across from her is eyeing Mr. Beefy. "Not in here," I say. "Let me grab someone to cover the front. We'll do this outside. And no need to come back and tell me the results. I know they'll be negative." I smile sweetly like the waitresses do around the annoying customers. "Wait for me out front. You're already drawing attention."

He laughs and shakes his head but heads for the front door, and I hurry to the back. No way in hell am I letting him take my DNA. I thought about submitting my DNA when everyone was doing it to trace their lineage, but after researching the risks, I decided not to. There is all kinds of crazy shit people can do with it.

I wave Trent over from where he's flipping patties. "It's slowing down, wanna head to the party?"

"Yeah, cool. Let me ask Lisa if she needs anything before I cut out."

"I already asked her," I lie. "She's good." I nod to the backdoor hoping Lilly doesn't come out of the break room to see me dipping out. "Let's go out this way. There's a bitchy girl I went to school with up front. I don't feel like dealing with her shit."

He laughs as he hangs up his apron next to all the others. "Okay, babe."

My heart pounds against my chest as I push open the back door. My gaze darts around the parking lot, and I breathe a sigh of relief that it's empty. I speed walk to Trent's car, not relaxing until he's unlocked the doors and we're both inside. Giving up my phone is a small price to pay for a quick escape.

CHAPTER 4

I pull my work shirt off, leaving me in a small gray tank. Trent sets the air conditioner to full blast as he pulls out onto the main road, and I direct the vents on my side to blow on my face. I'm ready for fall. The summer heat has been too much.

Trent puts his phone to his ear, talking to someone about meeting us at the party. Probably one of his loser friends. He likes to have them around all the time even though they all hit on me. They've even straight-up asked me to sleep with them. When I showed Trent the texts, he laughed it off saying it was a joke.

"Get in the back, Scott's getting in."

I hadn't noticed we stopped or that we were parked in front of Scott's dad's apartment. I climb between the front seats and drop into the back. Scott gets in and he and Trent begin talking about some new rap song I've never heard of. I'm not a big music person but when I do listen, I prefer metal.

We drive around the block to another one of Trent's friend's houses. Jacob climbs into the back with me, sitting in the middle so he can lean between the front seats and talk with Scott and Trent. Jacob fills most of the back with his tall and athletic frame. The air conditioner has his greasy hair flying around his face and the smell of body odor wafting toward me. I squash myself against the side of the car, trying to get away from the stench.

I'm ignored and forgotten for a few minutes before Jacob's hand lands on my thigh. His fingers inch higher before I swat his hand away and jab him in the ribs. Apparently, I didn't jab him hard enough because he chuckles low. Jacob is such an ass. He has a girlfriend that he cheats on constantly. A few months ago, I told her I walked in on Jacob with another girl. She didn't believe me and accused me of trying to break them up.

Trent parks, taking his time to get out of the car because he's busy talking to his damn friends. Scott's out and moves his seat forward so Jacob can scoot out. Only then does Trent finally realize he should do the same for me.

I take a deep breath, relishing in the crisp fresh air. It's peaceful here. If I ever buy a house, I'd want a place like this. Mine and Nana's houses are in busy subdivisions with constant noise.

All that can be heard here is the soft sound of music coming from the bottom of the hill where a medium-sized bonfire crackles. Danny lives with his parents in a small log cabin. The home is brushed up against the trees that surround the open property.

The fire lights the way as we head toward Danny's party shed where several people have gathered to play beer pong. Danny began construction on his shed a couple of years ago but never finished. Only one wall has drywall with a few blacklight posters tacked to it. The rest of the walls are bare wood that have been lazily painted dark blue. A worn gray couch sits against the back wall and a fridge is next to it. The ping pong table everyone is surrounding sits at the center of the room and is currently being used for beer pong.

I pull a beer from the fridge while Trent and Jacob talk with a group of people they know. My fingers keep going to the back of my neck thinking maybe I'll feel the thing Mr. Beefy claims is there.

I crack open the can and chug it. A few people cheer me on and that gets Trent's attention. He likes to be in the spotlight. He wraps his arms around my shoulders, pressing his chest against my back.

"Wanna play beer pong?" he whispers against my neck.

I shrug him off, moving to the fridge to grab another beer. "I think I saw Grace by the fire. I'll catch up with you later." Trent looks aggravated but his friends are calling him to start a new game, and his friends always come first. I crack open the second can and drain half of it before I make it to the fire.

When I picture a girl named Grace, I think of a blonde-haired, blue-eyed, church girl. My Grace is the opposite of that. Her hips are swaying to Marilyn Manson's "The Dope Show." I know his music gets a bad rap but it's the best to dance to. I like a beat that calls to me. This is one of my favorite songs to move to.

"You're here," Grace says, moving toward a red cooler next to a row of plastic chairs. She pulls out a beer, pops the top, and holds it out to me. "I didn't know you were coming."

I down the can in my hand, toss it into the fire, and then take the bottle she offers. "Had nothing else to do."

"I'm glad you came. I was bored as shit." She rolls her dark brown eyes. "Georgia's passed out inside. She lost at beer pong four times." She begins to sway to the music, moving closer to the fire. "I need a new dance partner."

I drain my beer and toss the empty bottle into the woods, disappointed when I don't hear it smash against a tree. I lift my arms into the air and close my eyes as I begin to move. I love to dance like this, slow and free.

After a few songs, Grace and I drop down to the plastic chairs and each grab a beer from her personal cooler. She always comes prepared.

She pushes shoulder-length black hair from her face. "You've been distant."

"I've been busy." I take a swig of beer and avert

my eyes, hoping she isn't going to try and have a "heart to heart." Grace is my only real friend and our friendship works because she isn't like other girls. Grace has a few friends we both hang out with, but I never hang out with them unless she's around.

"How's Tilly? You and her moved in with your grandmother, right?"

I take a sip of my beer, feeling a slight buzz from the other ones before this. "We moved in last week. Tilly's good. She has her days but for the most part she's good." I take another drink. "How's college? You still crushing on your Bio teacher?" I grin.

"Yep, I'm in love." She winks and lights a cigarette. "Were you able to enroll for fall classes?"

"No. Maybe next year." I shouldn't have brought up college. I down my beer and reach toward her cooler. "Mind?"

She waves me off. "Have at it. I have more in the car. Stole a few cases from my brother's girlfriend."

I grab a beer, quickly downing half of it. I want the alcohol to take me away, help me forget about this shit day. "Your brother still with that prissy bitch?"

She rolls her eyes and blows out a stream of smoke. "Yep. They moved in together."

"Hello, ladies." Jacob drops down next to Grace, and a few others come up behind him, taking seats on the empty chairs around us.

Not wanting to be social, I move to get up, but the fat blunt Jacob pulls from behind his ear stops me. Trent comes into view and asks the person on my left to move down so he can sit next to me. I wish he'd go away. Alcohol makes me like him even less than I already do. God, I'm a bitch. I can't keep doing this to him or myself.

I take the blunt Grace hands me, hitting it a couple times and then passing it to Trent. He ignores the puff puff pass unspoken rule, taking a few extra hits, and then passes it down the line. A couple of chairs down, I recognize a guy and girl I went to school with. I can't remember their names, but the girl takes a hit and coughs her lungs out.

I wait for the weed to get to me one more time before telling Trent I'll be back, and then I get up and make my way toward the lake at the edge of the property. It's peaceful out here with the crickets chirping and the sky full of stars above me. I drop down to the grass. The alcohol and weed have me feeling pretty good but what happened today won't seem to slip from my mind.

My fingers find my neck again. The skin there is silky smooth. I move my fingers into my hairline, not feeling anything there either. I down my beer, telling myself I'll deal with everything tomorrow. Tonight is my escape.

Ready to dance some more, I head back to the party. Grace, Danny, Jacob, and Trent are the only ones left at the fire. A small group of people lingers outside the shed. Some of the cars that were parked at the top of the hill are gone, so I'm guessing most people dipped out after the blunt.

"Where'd you go?" Trent asks, moving from the chair next to Jacob to meet me at Grace's cooler.

I grab a beer and pop the top. "For a walk."

He glances toward the direction I came from and shakes his head. "What's up with you lately?"

I want to smack him. He should know. My dad checked into rehab after turning to pain medication and alcohol to ease his suffering that was caused by my mom's death. I'll be twenty in a few months, and I have nothing to show for it. I have a shit job, no car, and I'm basically a mother to my fifteen-year-old sister. My life is fucking stressful right now.

I only got with Trent out of convenience. It isn't right to use someone like that. I don't really feel guilty about it, but at least I know it's wrong.

"Come here. Talk to me a minute." I lead Trent a few yards away from the fire, closer to Danny's house. "Okay, I think we both know this isn't working. You should move on." There, Mom would be proud of me for letting him down nicely. I don't know how I'll get to work but fuck it.

Trent jerks back like I slapped him. "Are you fucking serious?"

"Yeah, I am." I can't hold back my smile. Being with him felt like a ten-pound weight pressing against my chest. There's still weight there from other things, but I can breathe so much better now.

He spits to the side. "Fuck you, Hayley."

"Come on, Trent. I was a shit girlfriend. You're better off."

"Where the fuck is this coming from? Why are you being a bitch?"

I turn away, determined to be the bigger person, and because I don't feel like arguing with him, but he stops me by grabbing my arm and yanking me back a step. I glare at him and his hand falls away.

He flicks his head. "You're drunk. You need to sleep this shit off, and we'll talk in the morning."

I shake my head. "There's nothing to talk about. I might be drunk, but I've been thinking about this for a while."

"Whatever, bitch. You never put out anyway. Find your own ride home." He shoulder checks me causing some of my beer to spill down my arm.

I fight with myself not to throw the glass bottle at the back of his head for ramming his shoulder into mine so hard. I didn't think he'd be mad. He rarely acknowledges me anyway. When he's with his friends, it's all about them, and they are around ninety percent of the time.

Seeing an opportunity, Jacob slithers up to me, snaking his arm around my shoulders. This persistent motherfucker is getting on my nerves. A couple of years ago, I'd have kicked him in the balls and broken his nose the first time he touched me, but I'm trying to be better. My mom said violence isn't the answer, even though I think it is sometimes. Like now.

"Get off." I shove him away but only hard enough that he moves a step back.

"You and Trent finally over?" Jacob laughs. "You inflated his ego. Nobody understands why you got with him."

"What's that supposed to mean?"

"You're fine as fuck, and he's not." He points toward the shed with his chin. "Look at him trying to spit game to Kelsey. She's fine as hell. He never would have done that before you." He laughs. "Have you seen any of his ex-girlfriends? They are all ugly as fuck."

I don't look because I don't care. "Whatever. Trent can have whoever he wants."

"What about me? Can I have whoever I want, 'cause I've been wanting you." He reaches toward my face, and I lean away. "Let me have a taste, Hayley."

A dark shadow covers Jacob's face as a warm body moves behind me. I instantly tense up. I don't like that someone snuck up on me.

"Tell your boyfriend to get lost. He can have a taste later."

The guy behind me has a deep and raspy voice. It's one I don't recognize, and Jacob must not either because he says, "Who the fuck are you?"

I step to the side, turning to face the stranger. The hood from his black hoodie is up and pulled low, covering his eyes. I can see he has a strong jawline, full lips, and a straight nose. His shoulders are broad, and he's got an inch or two on Jacob.

"It doesn't matter who the fuck I am. Get lost," the stranger says, taking a step toward Jacob, and I back up three.

"Fuck that. I got here first," Jacob says, moving quickly behind me, his chest coming against my back.

This drunk idiot. I'm about to tell him to shut the fuck up when he makes a mistake. Slipping his arm around my torso, his thumb purposely brushes against the nipple of my left breast. I know it's not an accident because he does it again.

I rear my elbow back into his taut stomach as hard as I can. He grunts, and I whirl around to shove him back while he's unguarded and bent over. He stumbles to the side and then straightens, looking furious.

It makes me want to laugh. Jacob has always been an annoying asshole. Leave it to him to get mad at the girl he's always touching without permission. I've tried to be nice, using my words, but it never gets through to him.

"Fucking bitch." He raises his hand to either hit or grab me but the guy in the hood darts forward and grabs Jacob's arm, twisting it behind his back.

I hear his deep voice practically growl something and then he releases Jacob with a shove.

"Whatever," Jacob says, backing up. "I hear the bitch won't put out anyway." He storms away, leaving me alone with the stranger in the hoodie.

CHAPTER 5

"What do you want?" I tilt my head, trying to see under his hood but I can't. The shadow from his hood is blocking my view. His silence is making me impatient, so I give him my back and make my way toward Danny's house.

I reach for my phone to tell him I'm going to crash on the pull-out bed in his room, but my back pocket is empty. I grind my teeth, remembering my phone was taken. My hand grips the doorknob when the presence of someone behind me has me tensing.

"You trying to escape?" His rough voice is low.

I turn around to face him as his heavy body backs me up and cages me against the door. His arms shoot out on either side of my head. He towers over me, invading my space.

"I'm going inside to crash. Move."

The light of the fire is behind him, so he's covered in shadow while I'm bathed in light. I feel his gaze on my face. He's quiet like he's studying me. I'm about to kick him in the nuts when he says, "You have contacts in?"

I roll my eyes. I've been asked this before. "No, dude. I have perfect vision."

"To change the color of your eyes," he says, sounding aggravated.

"I said no." This dude is weirding me the fuck out. "You need to back up."

He leans in closer, bringing his hand to my face and gripping my chin. He's big, strong, and dominant. He is the opposite of Trent and definitely my type. The stranger's warm breath fans across my face. If he would have tried talking to me like a normal person, and not tried to intimidate me like he's doing now, I might have given him a chance.

I lift my arms between us and press my hands to his chest. I push against him, but he's too close for me to get enough leverage. "I said you need to back up."

His fingers release their tight hold of my chin. "You think being Anna will save you from your shit life?"

That sobers me up. "What the fuck?" *Did I say something out loud tonight about the interview?* "Who are you?" I attempt to push against him again, but it's more like I'm feeling him up. I let my arms drop back down to my sides.

He presses even closer, his mouth now at my ear. "The life of a Westling isn't as glamorous as you think. You'll be watched like a hawk by everyone. Anything and everything you do will be analyzed, dissected, and discussed by the media. You'll crack under pressure, probably by slitting your dainty wrists." He steps back, giving me breathing room and space to move.

I don't know how this dude found out what went down at the interview, and I can't see his face to know who he is. "You have the wrong person."

"Let me see the back of your neck."

"No. Go away, creep." I step around him, shoving him as I do.

A second later I'm spun around, my front pinned against the hard metal door. His whole body covers mine, making me ten times hotter than I was and not in a good way. I wince as his fingers probe and pull at the sensitive hair on the back of my neck.

As fast as he pinned me, I'm released. Breathing heavy, I slowly turn around. "Who are you?" I feel his eyes all over me, but I can't see them with that freaking hoodie. I want to rip it off.

"Tell me how you found out about the mark and I'll give you twenty-five thousand dollars."

"You'll give me twenty-five thousand dollars? You have twenty-five thousand dollars?" I think I'm more shocked about that than the fact he found out about the interview. He can't be much older than me and nobody my age has that kind of money. "Some dude named James brought up some crazy shit about a neck mark." I hold out my hand. "Where's my money?"

"No!" he barks. "Tell me who put it on the back of your neck."

"Put what? There's nothing there!" My anger's rising, threatening to bring me to the place where I lose control and my self-preservation disappears. It's a weird feeling. Sometimes I black out completely when I lose my shit. The last time that happened, when I came to, I was pinned under a security guard. Turned out, I had broken a girl's jaw. I was sent to alternative school after that. Whatever. School is school. They all suck.

"How'd you find out?" He backs up a step. "Is someone paying you to do this? Have you thought about the people you're going to hurt?"

"Are you drunk? Listen, I'm not Anna, and I haven't claimed to be, so you can go."

He chuckles low and deep. "So, you're trying to back out? Can't handle the pressure already?" He scoffs. "We'll find out who you're protecting, so tell me who gave you the tattoo."

"Tattoo?"

"Stop playing dumb. The tattoo on the back of your neck."

"I don't have a tattoo on my neck, you fucking idiot. What the fuck is really going on?" I look around, not seeing anyone nearby but it's getting harder to see because the fire is dwindling. "Is this a prank?"

"Is there a problem?"

I recognize his voice right away. I glare into the

night not seeing anyone at first. A second later, Mr. Beefy's large body comes into view. Now I get it. These two must work together. That explains the size of dark and dangerous in front of me. He's security.

"What are you doing here?" I throw the words at Mr. Beefy.

"Here to get that DNA swab. Think I wouldn't find you?"

"Hoped," I mumble. "And I don't consent to being swabbed."

Dark and dangerous laughs. "It's not about what you want anymore."

He moves fast, shoving me against the door harder than before. My shoulder hits first and hard. This asshole pins my body down with his. His large hand grips my face, squeezing my cheeks so hard I'm forced to open my mouth. He shoves a swab in and moves it around, not trying to be gentle.

We're not on anyone's radar way over here but if I were to scream, I'm sure someone would come to see what's going on. I don't scream, though. I'm afraid one of these two idiots will say something about their ludicrous suspicion. The swab hits the back of my throat making me gag and then his body leaves mine.

With my fists clenched, I spin around. "You can't do that!" I lunge for the swab, but he shuffles back a couple of steps.

"I can and did. Now, let's go."

"Go?"

"We're taking you home," the hooded jerk says.

I laugh. "I'm not going anywhere with you."

"We can't leave you here," he growls.

Sleeping at home is a much better choice than Danny's shit mattress on the floor, but I'm pissed off. I'd rather sleep in the yard than go anywhere with this guy.

"Don't you want your phone back?" Mr. Beefy says. "It's been making sounds. It might be important."

My mind instantly goes to Tilly. She could have tried calling me. "Of course I want my phone, asshole." I hold my hand out.

The hooded jerk knocks my hand away. "Don't be stupid. You know it's not gonna be that easy."

I glare at them. "Straight home. I have pepper spray, and I'm a black belt in karate, so don't try anything stupid." Neither of those are true.

"Whatever." The hooded jerk turns around and begins to walk up the hill.

"This way, Miss Westling."

"Don't call me that," I snap at Mr. Beefy. "You can't honestly think I'm Anna. It's fucking insane."

"I honestly do," he replies. and I feel sick and angry. Maybe I should have let him swab me in the beginning, then, this would already be over with. Well, I think it would be over with. I've never done a DNA test, but I'd assume the results would be quick like a pregnancy test.

"How long is this DNA test gonna take?" I watch

the hooded jerk bypass parked cars, heading toward a blacked-out SUV.

"Sometime tomorrow. Nick is insisting we use a laboratory in California instead of something local here where we would get the results a lot quicker."

"Nick?" I question.

"Dominick Cabot. He's been helping Aiden—"

"I know who Nick Cabot is. Wait, is that Nick?" I gesture to where the hooded jerk is moving into the passenger seat of the SUV.

"Yes."

My eyes widen and what's left of my buzz disappears. I stood up to Dominick Cabot, the broody asshole who put a handful of paparazzi in the hospital with his fists. The guy who "allegedly" led cops on a ten-mile chase on his Kawasaki Ninja H2R but it could never be proven because he escaped. The fucking guy who has been arrested more times than I can count for bar fights and DUI's.

A wide grin splits my face. I think I held my own for going up against a guy with such a colorful past. Maybe Dominick Cabot should fear me. I have quite the lengthy record of my own

"So, is Aiden here too?" I ask.

"No, Aiden isn't here." Mr. Beefy opens the back door on the driver's side and gestures for me to get in.

I peer into the back seat making sure nobody else is back there before I hop in. The seats are cream-colored and leather. Nick is in the front, arms crossed, and hood free. I can only see the side of his face, but damn, that's all that's needed to see how gorgeous he is.

It could help that I've committed him to memory, but not by choice. His face is everywhere. He's been on every cover of every magazine. His photos are plastered all over social media. Tilly even had a poster of him tacked to the wall in front of her bed. Some nights, when I'd sleep on her trundle bed because she didn't want to be alone, I'd fall asleep staring at that poster of Nick Cabot. This is so weird.

The overhead lights shut off leaving us in darkness when Mr. Beefy takes the driver's seat and closes the door.

"I'll take my phone back now." I reach my arm between the front seats, holding out my hand. "And don't you need my address?"

Mr. Beefy places my phone into the palm of my hand. "I have your grandmother's address. The one on the NDA was fake."

"Imagine that." I click my seatbelt into place as the SUV begins to move. "So, if you guys think I'm Anna, why isn't Aiden here?" I check my phone for missed calls and messages, but there aren't any. *Well played, Mr. Beefy.*

"You'd like that, wouldn't you? Get Aiden here and feed him a sob story. Try to get money out of him," Nick says from the front, not bothering to turn around and look at me.

I cross my arms and stare out the window. He can't even answer a simple question, but I think I get it. Aiden hasn't been informed Mr. Beefy thinks I'm Anna. No point in telling him or any other Westling without a confirmed DNA test.

My eyes start to feel heavy, but I keep them open. A stupid headache begins to form right as we pull up in front of my grandmother's. I push the door open and hop out. My bed is sounding really good right now. I pull the key from the frog statue's butt, unlock the door, and then stagger to bed.

CHAPTER 6

I'm dizzy when I peel my crusty eyelids open. It feels way too early to be awake, but my desert dry as fuck mouth and full bladder force me up. I creep out the room, careful not to wake my sister.

First stop is the bathroom and then I make my way to the kitchen. I pull open the fridge but shut it a second later. Everything in there needs to be cooked, and I don't feel like cooking. I guzzle a glass of tap water.

I would kill for tacos with extra taco sauce. Or chicken alfredo. That's one of my favorite meals. Pizza is a close second and spaghetti is third. My stomach growls loudly, probably pissed off I'm not giving it all of our favorite things. I wish the nearest McDonald's wasn't ten miles away or that Nana didn't meet her two best friends for coffee on Sunday mornings before church. I could totally go for a sausage biscuit and hash browns right now.

I step outside and am pleasantly surprised to find gray skies. I grab the plastic Tupperware container from behind the bushes next to the porch, and then I drop onto the mesh hammock at the side of the house. I pop the lid and inspect the contents to make sure nobody pinched anything from my stash.

Hoping the green will help me get back to sleep, I pull out a pre-rolled joint. The fresh air has me feeling a little bit better at least. I grab the black Bic from the container and light up.

It doesn't take long for me to smoke it down and drop the roach to the ground. The light breeze and blocked out sun has it feeling perfect out and not the ninety degrees it's been. It's cooler out here than it is inside. I let my lids close and my body relax. The soothing sounds of nature and my high help me drift to sleep.

***

"Are you fucking kidding me? Get up."

The deep baritone creeps into my mind, bringing me to a half-awake half-asleep state. I'm on the verge of slipping back under to dreamland when the sting to my thigh has my eyes popping open. Dark brown eyes and hair; a beautiful fallen angel towers over me. His shirt is gray like the sky behind him. The thin cotton stretches over the thick muscles of his arms. Nick Cabot stands above me looking every bit as gorgeous as he does in his pictures. Maybe even more so in person.

Nick Cabot is in my yard. Dammit. *Why couldn't last night have been a fucked-up trip from laced weed?* I narrow my eyes when I realize he just fucking slapped me. I rub the spot on my thigh that's turning pink. "What the fuck?" I growl.

"Did you actually fall asleep out here surrounded by paraphernalia? And what the fuck are you wearing?"

The contents of the Tupperware are on my stomach and the empty container is at my side. I quirk a brow. "Paraphernalia? Does this offend your royal highness?" I scoop up the offending *paraphernalia* and shove it back into the container. "And I have pajamas on."

"I can see your nipples."

I glance at my thin tank. It's black, so you can't actually see anything, but my bra-free nipples are pebbled from the fabric brushing over them and the cool breeze. "So. Everyone has nipples. What's the big deal?"

Nick's jaw clenches. "This is why you couldn't handle being Anna. If she were caught like this, the family name would be slandered."

I run my fingers through my tangled hair. "For smoking weed? It's almost legal everywhere now."

His eyes are cold as his lip curls in disgust. "You'd be a drug addict, passed out on the lawn, after a night of reckless partying."

I get to my feet. "Whatever. I don't give a fuck what people say about me."

He stops me from moving past him by stepping

into my path. "In this life, it's not all about you."

"Good thing I'm not a part of that life. Why are you here?" Behind him, Mr. Beefy is next to the SUV I rode home in. "What time is it?"

"I'm here waiting for the results. The swab made it to the lab an hour ago." His gaze moves to my legs and he clenches his jaw. "Your ass is hanging out."

I roll my eyes. I'm not even going to entertain that comment. "And again, why are you here? You can wait for the results somewhere else."

"You've already slipped away from James, twice."

"Whatever. Don't wait in the yard. Feel free to leave once you get the results."

He glares at me, his dark brown eyes almost black. "Still determined to protect whoever told you about the mark? What if I raise the offer to a hundred thousand?"

My dry mouth becomes even drier. That's a lot of money. I could pay for college and help my dad with bills. "Erin Reynolds." I instantly regret not asking to see the money first. My brain spazzed at the thought of having a hundred thousand dollars.

Nick waves Mr. Beefy over. "Run the name Erin Reynolds."

Mr. Beefy pulls out his phone, taps at the screen, and then holds it up to me. "Which Erin Reynolds?" He scrolls through the names showing me it's a really long list. "These are the ones in a sixty-mile radius."

"That one." I absently pick one.

Mr. Beefy chuckles. "Mrs. Erin Jane Reynolds. Her address puts her at the Sunny Days nursing home twenty-three miles away. She's been a resident for two years and recently celebrated her eighty-sixth birthday."

Nick grabs my upper arms. "Do you think this is a fucking game?"

His fingers dig into my muscles so hard it feels like he's going to crush them. I bite back a yelp as he squeezes even harder, and then I yank free and slap him across his perfect face. My eyes are wild and wide as I watch his whole face turn bright red. My hand stings, so I know his face has to. His nostrils flare and jaw clenches.

Oh shit.

Keeping my eyes on him, I back up, but he's quick and lunges. His arms wrap around my torso and lift me off the ground. He squeezes my back against his chest and begins walking swiftly toward their ride. I'm too stunned to do much about it.

"Let's go pay Mrs. Reynolds a visit at the nursing home. I bet the cops will want to speak with her for her crimes."

"Sir," Mr. Beefy says.

"Fuck off, James."

"Fine, you fucking asshole. I made it up! Let me go!"

I'm released, only to have my back pressed against the SUV's passenger side door as Nick's body covers mine. "Are you going to tell me a name or not? I don't play games."

We're both breathing heavily as our eyes lock. His body is twice the size of mine. Even if I did know karate, I don't think I could take him.

"Sir, Aiden is trying to reach you."

James's voice comes from close by, but I can't pull my eyes away from Nick's intense glare.

The way his jaw is locked tight makes me want to run my fingertips over his full lips to see if that might loosen him up. He said he doesn't like to play games. I think he doesn't know how fun they can be.

I'm not new to anger. I have my own demons coursing through my veins. For me, something thrilling, or sex can help bring me down. I wonder if Nick is the same? I bet he's good in bed. From what I've experienced, the angry ones are.

I'm probably fucked up for getting turned on by his anger and rage. My first relationship was intense, and according to my therapist, it was toxic. It was all about fighting and sex. The fighting made me feel crazy, and the sex made me feel high. I think we'd intentionally start fights to get to the sex. God, it was fucked up, and I'm fucked up for still craving it.

Our eyes are still locked, but my eyes begin to burn, so I blink. Somehow that feels like I lose. My gaze moves down to his lips, and I lick mine. The chaotic energy swirling around us has me feeling so alive. This was what it was like with my ex.

Toby was always rough with me when we'd argue. He'd pin me down to yell in my face. I hated the yelling, but the way he'd pin my wrists and press his body against mine, always made me crazy in a really good way. My shrink should have committed me. I'm fucked in the head.

"Fuck." Nick pulls his phone from his pocket and taps at the screen while bringing his forearm to my chest to hold me still. He doesn't move his dark eyes from mine which makes this so much hotter.

I'm sure any girl in my position would be turned the fuck on now too. Nick Cabot is uber fucking famous, rich, and fine as hell. He was voted hottest man alive last year in one of the girly magazines my sister reads. That helps me feel better about the way my body is reacting. My stupid nipples are straining against the fabric of my thin top and I'm wet, so damn wet.

Nick slips his phone back into his pocket and then angrily pulls it back out a second later while sneering at me. He puts it to his ear. "What?"

His voice is so fucking deep. That just adds to his attractiveness. If Trent was to manhandle me like this, I'd break his nose. Beautiful people really do have it easier in life, and Nick Cabot is as beautiful as they come. Fucking prick. Attractive and rich. Maybe I will break his nose. It's only fair.

He looks away from me. "You're sure? You ran the test yourself?"

My stomach clenches at the word test. This will

all be over soon. Nick Cabot pressed against my body will soon be a distant memory I will keep to myself.

"And Charles delivered it?" There's a tense pause, and then, his nostrils flare, and he says, "I understand."

For a moment he looks like he's going to explode, but then his gaze meets mine, and I watch as his demeanor completely changes. No longer is Nick Cabot the brooding and angry boy. The blood drains from his face, and with frantic eyes, and trembling hands, he shoves his phone back into his pocket.

He swallows and steps back a foot. "How?"

I don't like the feeling I have in my gut, but it could be from the lack of food and the fact he looks terrified. "What?" My voice comes out weak, so I say it again but louder.

He's as still as a statue as he stares at me. My heartbeat pounds against my chest. A car slowly drives by, loud music coming from it. That seems to break him out of whatever trance he was in.

His color slowly returns as does his anger. "You need to do another test," he growls. "Get in." He shoves me to the side and then rips the back door open. "We'll get another swab. There is no way you're her. No fucking way. You manipulated it somehow. We'll use a different lab."

I feel like my world is crashing down at his words. "What can I do to make you forget all this and walk away?"

His eyes narrow. "What?"

"It's clear you don't want me to be Anna. I don't want to be her. Pretend this never happened." I search his face, but I can't read anything besides anger. I have no idea what he's thinking, only that he's mad. "Please," I whisper, and he averts his eyes. "The test said I'm her?" *Please say no.*

"Yes," he grinds out, the muscle in his jaw flexing.

"Fuck. Nobody else knows, though? You don't have to tell anyone, please."

His gaze meets mine again. "Tell me who gave you the mark. Tell me how you pulled off the DNA test. Why have you changed your mind?" He pushes me back against the SUV, his hand on my shoulder, holding me against the cool metal. "Who the fuck are you working for?" When I don't immediately say anything, he brings his face closer to mine. "Tell me now or I will burn your fucking house to the ground with you inside." The grin that splits his face is wicked and deadly.

CHAPTER 7

I bet his words and cruel smile would work on most people. Threats usually do. But his over the top threat is unbelievable. Nick may be desperate for information, but I find it hard to believe he'd commit murder to get it. That, and I'm sure James wouldn't let him.

I push him back and he moves, giving me space. "I would love to tell you I planned all of this, but I fucking didn't. You have two options, walk away and pretend this didn't happen or move forward. I hope you choose to walk away."

He tugs at his hair, looking up at the sky and then back at me. "Fuck, what do you remember?" His frantic eyes search mine. "If you're Anna, you have to remember your family."

Stupid boy. I have had too many foster families. The memories are blurred and jumbled together. The people I'm told were my parents were not the Westlings. I shake my head.

"Think!" he shouts, his fingers digging into my

shoulders. "Tell me a memory!" Sounding desperate, he shakes me. "Anything!"

My forehead breaks out in a sweat. "I don't know! Eating runny eggs. Trying to fall asleep but a red light from the TV is shining in my face. The girl in the bed next to me won't stop snoring. The girl on the top bunk keeps crying. Riding my bike. Throwing up from being forced to eat broccoli. A foster brother being hit so hard blood from his nose sprays across my face. Being so hungry I feel like I'm going to die and still not getting fed." I shove him back as hard as I can. "Happy? There's some fucking memories for you!" I didn't mean to let all of that spill from my mouth, but I'm freaking the fuck out. My whole body is shaking as I storm toward the house, but I can't go in there like this. I'm on the verge of losing my shit.

I change course to walk down the road instead, but my legs give out. I fall to my knees in the grass. My heart is beating so hard against my chest I feel like if I don't slow it down, I'll have a heart attack. I plant my palms down onto the warm earth. I dry heave but nothing comes up because I haven't eaten since yesterday afternoon. Deep breaths. The birds are chirping. I feel the breeze against my legs. The sound of a car horn blows a few streets over. Deep breaths.

Strong arms haul me up. Closing my eyes, I let my head fall back against a shoulder. The sound of an airplane. Footsteps scraping over pavement. Deep breaths. Normally I use this tactic so I don't break everything around me but I'm using it now so I don't pass out. I open my eyes as I'm set down onto something soft. I'm in the back of the SUV with the door open and Mr. Beefy hovering over me. He wipes sweat from my face with a white cloth. Nick is in the front seat of the SUV, arms crossed and quiet.

"Do you need to go to the hospital?"

I wave him away and shake my head. He eyes me warily while I take a minute to catch my breath and slow my heart. "I need... just move, please." I step past him to pull the passenger door open. "What happens now? What did you decide?" I need to know what my next step is.

"Aiden's on his way. It's up to him now." Nick's jaw works. "I swear to God, I hope you understand what this will do to him. You have thirty minutes to grow a conscience."

Fuck. I was hoping he'd do the right thing and walk away. My shaking legs carry me inside where Tilly is lying in bed scrolling through her phone. I move to our shared dresser and begin to pack a bag.

"I have to go, and I can't explain why. I want you to come with me, but if you don't want to, you can stay here with Nana," I say in a rush.

"What? You're leaving? Like for good?" She quickly pulls on shorts under her baggy pajama shirt.

"I don't know how long, probably a while. Think fast. I need to be gone in five."

"Where?" She grabs her bag and begins to shove clothes into it.

I grab the safe and pull out all my cash, shoving it into my bag. "I don't know. Maybe Uncle Ben's place at the lake? Yeah, I think there. We can take the bus most of the way, Uber the rest."

"What happened?"

I slip on my Vans. "I'll explain later. Ready?"

She nods, throwing her backpack over her shoulder and heading for the front door, but I grab her wrist and nod toward the laundry room. "Back door."

"Your clothes."

"Shit." I hurry back to the room and change into jeans and my Live Free or Die tank, leaving the pajamas on the floor.

A second later, we're out the back door and climbing over the fence. Tilly is my ride or die. I love that she doesn't know what's going on but she's by my side regardless. We move through the neighbor's back yard and then onto the street.

"I don't even know where a bus station is. The cabin's only a little over an hour away. We can Uber." I pull my phone from my pocket and freeze with my finger over the app. Trey recently started working for Uber. I swipe over to the search bar. Taxi it is.

Tilly brushes her wispy bangs from her eyes. "That's gonna be crazy expensive."

Finding the number, I say, "I can make more money. It's fine." I call the taxi service, give them our location, and then hang up. "They're gonna have a driver call me back with the estimated time."

"Are you running from someone?"

My phone rings from a number I don't recognize. "Hello?"

"Where are you?"

My eyes widen and I hang up. That wasn't the cab driver. "Come on." I begin a quick pace down the sidewalk. "We need to get a little farther."

"Okay, but I wish I knew what was going on. Want me to call Margo? Her mom doesn't normally let her drive alone, but she might be able to talk her into it. Maybe she could take us to the lake."

At the end of the street, I look both ways before making a left. "Maybe. Give me a minute."

The same number lights up my phone again. I hit ignore. Nick Cabot is stupid if he thinks I'm going to speak to him. A week ago, I would have bet a million dollars I'd never meet him. Not only have I met him, I know what it feels like to have his body pressed against mine. I know he faintly smells of sandalwood and lemongrass, and he's fiercely loyal to his friend.

"They think I'm Anna," I mumble.

Tilly stops walking, catching my wrist. "What?"

I twist loose. "Keep walking or I stop talking."

She rolls her eyes but moves her feet. "Who thinks you're Anna?"

I tense as a car rolls by, but then relax as I see the driver is an old woman. "That security guard at the interview, and... Nick Cabot," I mumble Nick's name. "They're outside of Nana's house."

"Oh. My. God. No way!"

"Move those feet!" I snap.

She does, but she's grinning from ear to ear and not walking nearly as fast. "Are you serious? Of course you are or we wouldn't be running. Is Aiden here? He thinks you're Anna? Is that why you ran from the interview?" She stops walking again. "They didn't want you to take off your clothes, did they?"

"No, they didn't," I confess. "And they did a test. It might have said I'm Anna, but—"

Tilly's scream echoes around the neighborhood, and I knew I should have waited to tell her until we were at the secluded lake. An older man peeks his head out of his door to see what's going on. I drag Tilly farther down the sidewalk to stand under the shade of a tree.

Her blue eyes are wide. "We have to go back! This changes everything. I knew it! I told you!" She wraps her arms around my waist, crushing me against her.

I pry her off. She has no idea what this means. Tilly is probably picturing luxurious trips, shopping sprees, and fancy restaurants. What she isn't thinking is these people will want to have a relationship and those take lots of time and interaction. We live in Tennessee and they live in California. "Exactly, this changes everything," I say. "And not in a good way. Our whole family will be questioned by the police. Dad can't handle that right now. They may even arrest him."

Tilly's smile disappears. "But they adopted you. He didn't kidnap you."

I glance down at my phone and ignore another call from Nick. "He'll still be questioned. Dad doesn't need any added stress."

"Hayley." Tilly's eyes soften. "They are your family. You have a family. Stop thinking about all the bad that could happen and think about the good."

The small amount of good is pointless when there's so much more bad. "I already have a family. You and Dad are my priority. He can't deal with this right now. He hasn't been there long and it's a three-month program. He needs more time."

Tilly adjusts the bag on her back. "Maybe the cops would respect that and wait?"

"This is high profile shit, Tilly. People are going to want answers. Everyone will be interrogated." That has my heart rate picking up. Foster care was traumatizing. I finally quit having nightmares and flashbacks. I don't want anything to resurface. Anna Westling was only three when she was taken. They can't expect her to remember much. "They could have reported the wrong result, or maybe there was a mix-up."

"Do you remember anything? You were so little, but maybe if you concentrated you could remember them."

"There are only pieces of different families. I thought all of them were foster homes. It's possible that—"

The roar of an engine, and my sister's dropped jaw, has the blood draining from my face. I look over my shoulder and see Nick jumping out of the slow-rolling SUV. Nick's eyes are trained on me as he crosses the street, not bothering to check for oncoming traffic. Such a stupid and entitled thing to do.

CHAPTER 8

Now that the shock of meeting Dominick Cabot has worn off, my true feelings are emerging. Or maybe I'm just pissed off he chose to fuck my life up instead of walking away. My hands ball into fists at my side. I'm going to break his nose.

My sister stands dumbstruck as Nick steps up onto the sidewalk next to me.

"Where are you going?" He looks up and down the street. "Meeting someone?" He focuses on Tilly, eyes narrowing.

I step in front of my sister. I don't like the angry look he's giving her. "I'm leaving. You should let me. We both know nothing good can come from this."

"You made your choice when you refused to tell me a name." Nick's nostrils flare as his gaze moves to a sleek black car that's slowly approaching. In my gut I know that's Aiden. The car parks behind the SUV and James walks over to it.

Tilly snaps out of her stupor by shrieking, "You're Nick! Nick Cabot!" She shakes my arm. "Nick Cabot is here!"

Ignoring her, I focus on the boy getting out of the back seat of the black car. He's tall and lean like his pictures on TV, but instead of the darkness that usually clouds his eyes, I see light. The driver and James chat while Aiden and I stare at each other. Tilly's shrieking louder now because she sees Aiden too. Someone is probably going to call the cops. I should stop her, but I can't stop staring at the boy who's approaching.

"I hope you suffer for this," Nick hisses at me right before Aiden steps onto the sidewalk.

God, our eyes are the same. The exact same. Sapphire eyes so deep blue they could almost pass for purple. It's like looking into my own eyes.

"Hey," Aiden says, his voice barely above a whisper.

I think I say it back but Tilly's still yelling.

"Can we talk?" Aiden asks.

I clear my throat. "Um, over here." I gesture down the sidewalk, and he nods. "Don't talk to my sister," I throw over my shoulder to Nick but he's already on his way over to the SUV.

Once we're a good ten feet away from Tilly, I stop.

"You're Anna," Aiden whispers.

I see hope shining in his eyes. He thinks he's found his twin sister. "That's what Nick said, but I think there was a mistake with the test. I should do another one."

"James and Nick said you have the mark on the back of your neck."

I sigh. "There isn't anything on my neck. My sister checked."

Aiden's brows dip. "Can I look?"

I'm about to tell him no when I roll my eyes and nod. I lift my hair and give him my back. "See? Nothing there. Sorry you came all this way." I feel his fingers probing into my hair.

"It's there." I hear the click of a camera and then he's holding up his phone for me to see.

I stare at the image on the screen. It's hard to see detail because there's hair in the way but I see black swirling lines. It's small, about the size of a dime. Tilly must not have looked high enough because the mark is pretty far up into my hairline.

"He said it was a tattoo," I murmur. "Is that a cursive W?"

"It is," Aiden says. "The royal family marks their children when they are born."

This is bad. I glance at Tilly. She smiles and gives me a thumbs-up, and I shake my head in frustration.

"Let me see yours," I say, moving behind him. I stand on the tips of my toes to brush his wavy hair to the side to see the hint of a line. His hair is thick like mine and a shade darker. I use both hands to separate his hair enough to see more clearly. There it is. It's exactly like mine. It's even faded like an older tattoo would be. "Shit," I whisper.

Aiden runs his hand over the back of his hair, smoothing down the waves. "Are you okay? Do you want some water?"

I narrow my eyes. "What the hell is water going to do?" I shake my head. I'm not mad at him but I am angry. "Listen, Aiden, I'm sorry but you need to go. I can't deal with this right now. If you want to give me your number maybe I can text you sometime in the future."

"This isn't going how I imagined meeting you would go. You want me to leave?"

I nod. "Yes. I don't know how that mark got there, but I'm not Anna. I can't be."

"The test says you are. My—our parents are flying in and expecting to meet with you at my hotel."

"Why would you tell them to fly here? This is a mix-up. This happened to you before."

"A local lab was used in that case and the tech knew the girl being tested. She purposely falsified results, and she's in jail. We used a lab back home this time, and everything about you says you're Anna, my sister. I know it sounds weird, but I feel it."

"What about her mark? Did she have one too?"

"She had a tattoo on her shoulders that extended up onto her neck. James and I thought it was possible the original mark could have been covered so we ran a DNA test." He sighs. "If you don't come with me, they'll come here. Nothing is going to stop our parents from seeing you."

76

We stare at each other. I'm keeping my face expressionless but inside I'm freaking the fuck out. Things are moving too fast. Fucking typical me, ignored the problem hoping it would go away. I should have run to the cabin straight after the interview. Apparently being a procrastinator can ruin your whole life.

Aiden scratches his jaw. "If you'd rather them come here, I can ask." He frowns. "My mom doesn't like to change things last minute."

I can't hide the horror from my face. That is the worst idea ever.

"Is there a problem, Aiden?"

James strolls up, stopping next to Aiden and taking us in. Tilly thinks she can butt in as well and steps next to James with wide, hopeful eyes.

"Why hold the stupid interview thing when you could have announced on social media for every girl to check the back of her fucking neck for a tattoo?" I hiss.

"Because millions of girls would be tattooing the back of their neck, claiming to be Anna. And it's frowned upon to tattoo your child," Aiden says.

"What's going on?" Tilly asks. "What tattoo?"

"I need to change before going with you," I tell Aiden and then grab Tilly by the wrist. "This is so ridiculous," I mumble as I storm down the sidewalk with my sister.

"I can't believe you weren't going to tell me, and it's not ridiculous, Hayley. Your birth parents

77

were never found. It was like they vanished, which isn't possible. Now we know their names and your birth certificate are fake." Tilly snickers. "You're only eighteen."

I glare at her so hard. "I'm almost twenty."

"Anna and Aiden had their eighteenth birthday back in March."

"My ID says otherwise." I grit my teeth like I can make all of this go away if I want it hard enough. "I'm nineteen."

"Hello, girls!" Ms. Barbra calls from her front lawn.

Tilly waves but I pretend not to notice the old bat as we hurry past her house before she invites us up for cookies like she did the other day. She's a shit cook.

"I remember my parents, Tilly. They were real."

"You remember some people you were told were your parents. That doesn't mean they were your parents. Do you think they were the people who took you?"

"I don't know. It's not like I'd be able to give a description of them. The memories are hazy."

"The whole investigation CPS did was shady as hell. Why didn't they try harder to find them?"

I roll my eyes. "You know how they are. They don't put effort into the kids."

"My social worker was nice from what I remember. Why don't you want to be Anna? What are you scared of?"

I chew the inside of my cheek. Why don't I want

to be Anna? Isn't it every orphaned girl's dream to find her family? I was always told my parents were shit bags. I didn't want to find them. Finding a sibling or distant relative would have been cool, but I don't want this. Tilly doesn't understand.

"Hayley?"

I snap out of my thoughts. "I like the way things are. The Westling family has money but are they happy? Do they look happy in pictures? And what about Dad, Til? He doesn't need this right now."

She frowns. "We won't tell him until he's done with the program."

"What about you," I say. "If I'm Anna, are they going to want me to live with them? I'm sure they will want me to spend a lot of time at their home."

Tilly looks down at her feet. "Oh, I didn't think about that." She brushes her bangs to the side. "But I'll be fine here if you want to live with them."

She and I have never been apart for more than a day or two, and Tilly has separation anxiety. She's only been able to spend the night at her friend Margo's house who she has known for almost ten years. "I'm not going to live with them. I'm an adult, so they can't force me. But see what I'm saying, it's complicated. Everything would change." Her and I have had enough changes in our lives.

"I want you to be happy. I thought finding your family would help." She frowns, and I wrap my arms around her outside of Nana's house.

"I'm happy, Tilly. I don't have the excess happiness you have, and Mom had, but I'm okay."

"I thought finding your real mom would help. I wish we were home."

I pull her up the lawn to the front porch. "What, you sick of sharing a room with me?"

She laughs. "Kinda, but being home helps me remember Mom better. All her stuff is there. Her book is still on the table, opened to the page she was on. It smells like her there."

I tuck a lock of hair behind her ear. "It's not going to be like that for long. The rehab place wants Aunt Kathy to put Mom's stuff into boxes in the closet. It's not healthy for Dad or us to live like that. It's almost been a year."

"I know, and I want Dad to get better. He loved her so much. He's heartbroken."

"He'll get better."

"Mom's his soulmate. He said she was his forever. How do you get over that kind of loss?"

Pulling open the front door, I sigh, wishing our parents would not have put that soulmate bullshit into my sister's head. Her idea of falling in love with the perfect man is going to wreck her one day. That shit does not exist. And from my experience, guys suck. The ones our age anyway. They all want to party and fuck, no strings attached. Not that I necessarily want to be tied down. I know the guys I date now won't be my forever. But a healthy monogamous relationship would be nice. Most of us are too fucked up to have that, though.

Tilly and I head to our shared room where she

drops down on her bed and hugs her knees.

I throw my tangled hair into a messy bun. "I have to meet Aiden's parents real quick. I won't be long."

"Wow. You're going to meet your parents. The famous Westlings are your parents. This is pretty insane." Her voice rises an octave higher with each sentence.

I frown. "I'm not believing anything until I get a confirmatory test."

Tilly sighs loudly as I walk out of the room. In my frustration, I slam the front door a little too hard on my way outside. I've always had a hard time controlling my emotions and all emotions lead to anger. With Mom gone, it's been worse. I tried hard to be better for her. She always saw the best in me. She was blinded by love, but I love her for seeing me the way she did.

I groan. Trent's beat-up heap of metal is blowing exhaust fumes on the side of the street. He shuts it off when he sees me and hops out. He has the worst timing.

"Hey, babe." He lights a cigarette and leans against the trunk. "Feeling better today? You were a little crazy last night."

I'm a few feet away from him at the end of the driveway. "I meant what I said last night, Trent. It's over. We're both better off."

"Come on, babe." He steps up to me, his face softening. "I know things have been shit, but we'll get past that. Let's go for a ride. We can go back to my place, and I'll bend you over and fuck that pussy the way you like."

I shove him back and he laughs. "Just what every girl wants to hear, Trent."

"Oh, come on, Hayley. You ain't the flowers and chocolate kinda chick, and I'm not that kind of guy."

I pop a brow. "Oh yeah? What kind of girl am I, Trent?"

He winks. "The kind that likes to get on her knees. The type that likes to ride a man until he comes so hard he sees stars."

I laugh because he wants me to be that type of girl. The type that's all about *his* pleasure. "Fuck off, Trent. You don't know what kind of girl I am."

He flicks his cigarette to the side. "Jacob said you fucked some other dude last night. Is that what this is about? You been fucking someone else? 'Cause you sure as shit ain't been fucking me. You've barely let me into your fucking jeans since we started this." He steps closer, bringing his chest to mine and the smell of smoke and ash. "What the fuck's been up?"

Trent's eyes widen, and his shoes scrape across the concrete as Nick drags him backward by the back of his shirt like he weighs nothing. To the right, Aiden and James are moving my way. Nick deposits Trent by his car and glares down at him.

"What the fuck?" Trent brushes his shirt down and snaps his gaze to me. "This him? This the motherfucker you been fucking behind my back?"

Aiden moves to my side and James hovers a few yards away like Trent is a threat or something.

"You need to go, Trent," I say, hoping he doesn't recognize Aiden or Nick and blab they were here to everyone.

"Fuck this. You ain't shit." Trent storms back to his car and peels out, leaving an angry black mark and a cloud of smoke.

"Boyfriend?" Aiden asks and Nick glares.

I cough, clearing the air with my hand as I watch Nick walk back over to the SUV and climb into the passenger seat. "Ex."

"Is he going to be a problem?" Aiden asks, and I shake my head. He rubs the back of his neck. "Okay. You ready then?"

"No, but I don't have much choice." James holds the back door open for me and I climb in. "I'm going to need you to run through a drive through. I'm starving."

CHAPTER 9

Nick and James are in the front seat and Aiden and I are in the back as we zip down the freeway. I chew on the last fry, mad that I've eaten all the food and my greedy stomach's still growling.

"Dad said Liv's excited to meet you," Aiden says.

"Who?" I ask, setting my Coke in the cup holder between us.

He shakes his head. "Sorry, our sister. Liv is five."

I have a sister; her name is Tilly. I wonder if Aiden knows that? Did James tell him the things he read on whatever file he was able to pull up online? Does everyone in this vehicle know I was diagnosed with selective mutism at five, ADHD at seven, and ODD at eight? Did they read about the numerous fights I've been in? Do they know how bad my insomnia is or why I have it? Do they realize I'm nothing like them? If they did, I probably wouldn't have been invited to meet the famous Westling family.

Then again, they let Nick Cabot into their circle.

I pull at my lip ring. "What happens after the hotel?"

"I don't know. Mom and Dad didn't say."

I glance at a text from my sister. She sent me a bunch of smiley face emojis. She probably thinks this will be a happy reunion. John and Nora Westling are not just famous, they are world-renowned celebrities and to top that off, royalty. Nora Westling is a fucking princess.

I glance at Aiden as he sits perfectly poised in the seat. Everything about him is perfect. His flawless, wavy brown hair resembles plastic, and his golden skin is smooth and unblemished. His clothes look new, expensive, and preppy. And then there's me. My hair is greasy because I haven't washed it in three days, my lip and nose are pierced, and I have no posture.

I try matching Aiden's stance and it's uncomfortable as hell. I slouch back in my seat, rolling my eyes at how stupid this is. The famous family was searching for a perfect princess and dug up a deviant instead.

"I'm going to need a second test, and I can't stay long. I have a shift in a few hours."

"You want another test?" Aiden asks. "And what do you mean, a shift?"

"Yes, another test. And a shift... work. I'm a hostess at a restaurant."

He nods, shifting uncomfortably. I bet he'll

never have to work. I want to be mad at him for that, but it's not his fault. I'm jealous. Being an adult has shown me how hard it is to make it without money.

"Everyone's excited to see you," Aiden says. "I'm not sure how much you pay attention to news articles about us, but Colt's filming in California. He's our younger brother. He knows we found you and is going to try to fly in tomorrow. I'm sure Mom and Dad have called our extended family. Everyone will want to meet you."

I don't like hearing that. I'm picturing women gushing over me with smiling faces. There will be hugs and questions. I'm not good at pretending or lying to make others feel better. This is going to be awkward.

"You're living with your... Who did you say it was?" Aiden asks.

"My grandmother. My mom died last year. My dad isn't coping well with that. She was everything to him. He's working on himself, so my sister and I came to stay with his mom. She was the only relative in our area. I didn't want Tilly to be taken away from her friends."

Nick scoffs, the only sound he's made so far, and I clamp my mouth shut. I have no idea why I vomited up all that information.

"That must have been hard, losing your... losing her."

"It was hard. She was the absolute best." I don't miss that he didn't call her my mom. "She and

Tilly have huge personalities. They're full of kindness, they're sickeningly bubbly, and have more than enough positivity for a single person. I've never been able to match up to her, but she loved me regardless." I shake my head realizing my mistake. "Had. My mom had a huge personality." I twist my lips to the side. Shit. I did it again. I move my gaze out the window, hoping he won't ask me any more questions. I've never had a word vomit problem before.

Our eyes meet again and my stomach churns. There's something familiar about Aiden, and I guess if I'm Anna, there would be. Anna spent the first three years of her life with him and of course the nine months they were smashed together in a womb. "Did your parents ever find out why Anna was taken?"

"They assume money. Dad received a ransom call. He was cooperating with the kidnappers, but a couple weeks later he stopped hearing from them. There were no leads." He frowns. "Do you remember us?"

"I don't remember much before I went to live with my parents," I say, but not remembering much is a matter of perspective. I remember way more than I could ever want to.

"I'm glad you had good parents. Sometimes at night, my mind would come up with worst-case scenarios, and I wouldn't be able to sleep. I've worried so much." He frowns. "Seeing you now almost doesn't seem real."

I study his face. The dark circles under his eyes are more prominent in real life than they are in pictures although they were there too. Tabloids talked about drug use. I could see the lost look in Aiden's eyes, the way he was never quite focused on anything. I'm just now understanding what that look was. I had that look after my mom died. I guess for Aiden, it was different. I knew my mom was gone, but Aiden didn't know what happened to Anna. It would be hard to move on from that.

"My parents gave me a good life," I say, hoping it helps.

He glances at James. "James dug into your past. He said you'd been in foster care prior to adoption?"

I knew it. Aiden probably read whatever James found on me. "Yeah. A few different ones."

The SUV shuts off and my nerves kick-off which is a strange feeling for me. I'm rarely nervous, at least not to this extent. My palms begin to sweat, and my heart seems to be fluttering or some shit.

Aiden opens his door and pauses. "You don't need to be nervous."

"I'm not nervous," I say more harshly than I meant to, and I don't wait to see Aiden's reaction. I hop out of the SUV and stare up at the Westin Hotel. I've seen this hotel out the window while driving by. The entire building is made of windows that shine like gold when the sun hangs low in the sky.

I follow behind Aiden, James, and Nick as we

walk up the concrete steps and then through the glass doors. The front desk and lobby are unreal. A glass fireplace separates the front desk area from the wide-open lobby. Everything is decorated in different shades of gold and brown. The furniture looks expensive and new.

"Dad's panicking because he wanted to book one of the conference rooms. He says my suite is too small. He's excited to meet you. He wants it to go smoothly."

My stomach twists. What the hell is this feeling? I don't like it. "Whatever works." I shrug.

On our way to the elevator, we pass well-dressed men and women as they zip about, most of them busy with their phones. Nobody seems to notice Aiden Westling or Nick Cabot. Maybe these people are used to seeing the rich and famous.

We shuffle onto the elevator where a man and woman are having a heated conversation about something they forgot in their room. They snap their mouths shut as the doors close but the tension in the air is thick. It's making whatever emotion I'm feeling escalate. I think I feel guilt. Is that it? Maybe I feel guilty I'm about to disappoint these people.

Anna Westling is the daughter of a princess, for fuck's sake. Shit, am I a princess? I'm lightheaded and nauseous. I probably smell like sweat and weed. I didn't have time to shower. I feel grimy.

"It's not too late to put an end to this," Nick whispers next to my ear.

I narrow my eyes but don't say anything. He's wrong; it is too late to end this. Nick's thinking conspires when he should have been trying to find a way to get me out of this. We both don't want me to be here.

Our elevator companions exit on the fifth floor, but we continue up, stepping out a few levels below the top floor. My feet slow as Nick stops at a door on the right side of the hall, but Aiden gestures me forward.

"Let me know what the plan is," Nick says as he slides the card into the card reader.

"I will," Aiden says, as Nick slips into the room.

We pass a few more doors before stopping at a door on the left. My hand darts out to wrap around Aiden's wrist before he can swipe his card only to quickly release him and mumble an apology. I clench and unclench my fist at my side.

Aiden pauses with his hand on the handle. "Everyone's excited to see you. You don't need to be nervous."

"I didn't expect this. I thought I was there because my sister wanted to interview." I clear my throat. "I'm still having a hard time believing this."

"You have the mark and the DNA. You are my sister." His smile is wide and perfect.

I look into his eyes, mine swirling with emotions. His whole face is lit up, like today is the best day of his life, and maybe it is. How ironic it's one of the worst days of mine.

CHAPTER 10

Aiden gestures for me to go first, but I shake my head. There is no way I'm walking into that room first. I'd prefer not to go at all. James lingers down the hall. I wonder if he'd stop me if I ran out of here right now?

I don't get time to think about it because the door clicks open. Sucking in a breath, I follow Aiden into a sitting room. A large window overlooking the city takes up the far wall, a blue sofa is to the left, and two blue chairs face each other with a table between them.

There are only a few feet between the chairs and the couch where Mr. and Mrs. Westling sit. This is going to be an up-close and personal experience. I think I would have preferred the conference room Mr. Westling was trying to secure.

"Boo!"

A little girl with long blonde hair and white dress jumps out from the en-suite bedroom. Giggling, she leaps into Aiden's arms.

"You got me," he says playfully, setting her back on her feet.

Her round, blue eyes sparkle as she takes me in. Her little nose wrinkles, and her cheeks indent with adorable dimples as her smile widens. I can't help but smile back. She waves to me and then skips over to the table where a coloring book is lying open with a box of crayons next to it.

My gaze drifts to the well-dressed man and woman sitting side by side with their hands clasped tightly together. Nora Westling is wearing a silky, pale blue dress. Her blonde hair is tightly pulled back into a low, off-center bun. Her shoulders are tense, and it looks like she's holding her breath. John Westling's brown hair is almost black and his skin a warm gold. He has rich brown eyes and right now they are red and glossy.

The air in the room seems to get sucked out as we take each other in. My eyes feel wide like they are going to pop out of my damn head, and my heart is pounding against my chest. These people might be my parents, and they aren't ordinary people. I've seen John on TV shows and in movies. Nora has modeled for some of the top fashion designers around the world.

"Hey, bunny," Mr. Westling says, breaking the silence. "I used to call you that." He laughs. "You went through a rabbit phase. You acted like a bunny for weeks until..." A tear slips from his eye and trails down his cheek.

His lip quivers and then he's falling apart. Normally I feel awkward when people cry, but right now, I feel like crying too. Watching him cry like this brings back memories of my dad mourning my mother. He cried every day. I had never seen anyone so broken.

The little girl moves from the floor to run over to her distraught dad. She climbs onto his lap and rests her head against his chest. He rubs her back while wiping away his tears.

"Come have a seat, Anna." Nora gestures to the chair next to her but my legs only take me as far as the chair next to John.

She doesn't seem fazed by her husband's display of emotion. I would expect her to at least try and comfort him.

"Aiden, why don't you call room service and order drinks. What would you like, Anna?" Nora's form is formal, robotic.

I open my mouth to correct her about my name but change my mind. "I don't need anything." I rub at a stain on my jeans and shift in the stiff chair.

"Liv, come color Anna a picture," Nora says.

"Okay," Liv says, scooting off John's lap to plop down next to the table. "I'll color Daddy one too." She pulls her coloring book and crayons to the floor and lies on her stomach in front of them.

"Can I give you a hug?" John says, through a hoarse voice.

"Sure," I say, getting to my feet because how can I deny him a hug from his daughter who he hasn't seen in over a decade. I'd be a cold bitch if I said no.

He doesn't hesitate to wrap his arms around me, squeezing tightly, and I find myself hugging him back.

Smiling, he holds me at arm's length. "You look so much like Aiden." He chuckles softly. "What do you think, Nora? Did you think they'd look this similar?"

Nora smiles tightly. "Of course, they're twins."

"Where did you come from? Are you Anna? Daddy said you were." Liv says, looking up from her book.

John and I take our seats. "I was at my grandmother's house, and I was told I'm Anna. I don't remember being her," I say truthfully.

" 'Cause bad people took you when you were little?" Liv says, scribbling over the page with a red crayon.

"Yeah, but I wasn't with them for long. I found a family to take care of me."

John clears his throat. "I'm told you were adopted?"

I nod. "Not long after I turned twelve."

"It's probably unlikely they knew you were Anna, then," he says. "So much time had passed since you were taken."

"My mother was a saint. There was zero chance she was involved."

John reaches over and takes my hand. "I heard she died. I'm sorry for your loss."

I'm about to thank him but Nora cuts in, and says, "Yes, and her husband is in a rehab facility?"

I release John's hand. "He hit bottom when my mom died. He just needed some help dealing with it."

Nora nods. "Of course." Her gaze lingers on my pierced nose and then moves to my clothes.

There it is, the disgust I was waiting for. She doesn't like my look.

"What kind of things are you into? Do you play sports?" John asks.

I grimace because being adopted by two sports-oriented people could have been a disaster. Thankfully, my parents were all about being yourself and finding your passion. "No sports. I like writing and graphic art. My mom was an art teacher. She passed her passion on to my sister Tilly and me."

"Nora is an artist too. You'll have to see her work," John says, smiling and Nora frowns. "We have an art studio at one of our vacation homes. You'll love it."

I swipe my tongue over my front teeth. "About that. I'm not sure what you guys want to happen. How does all this work? I live in Tennessee, and you guys live in California. It's a long commute, and I should probably do a second test."

The room goes silent, everyone seeming confused, and then John says, "We're here to take you home."

My first reaction is to say hell no, but my mother raised me better than that. She always told me to put myself into other people's shoes. I need to try and show compassion. "I was thinking we could get to know each other while I live with my grandmother. I have a job, my sister to take care of, my dad will be out of rehab in a couple months, and I'm almost twenty—an adult."

"Eighteen," John says, with a reassuring smile. "You're eighteen."

My pulse kicks up a notch. If I'm a year and a half younger than what I've thought… I shiver. That's fucking weird.

"And you're our daughter. You should be home with your family."

"My grandmother and my sister are my family," I say, feeling angry he isn't considering my needs. I am fully prepared to walk out of this room and never see these people again. I will be doing it my way. They can't expect me to drop my life for them, but then again, they are probably used to getting their way in life. "I'm sure we can work something out," I say, not really believing it.

"Anna, come speak with me in the other room." Nora stands on high heels that put her a few inches taller than me.

Smiling, she takes my arm in hers and leads me into the en-suite. She leaves me by the bed while she walks over to the floor to ceiling window.

She stares out at the view. "My husband has been through too much to lose his daughter again. And Aiden—" She sighs, turning to face me. "He was devastated by the loss of his sister and then again by a con artist." Her eyes narrow, and her tone turns harsh. "You cannot come here and expect to gain the benefits of Anna without stepping into her role. I will not allow it. I will not have my family lose her all over again. It would be too much for them."

I study her pinched face. Not once did she mention how she felt or that she wanted Anna back. "Listen, I didn't ask for this—"

"You did," she snaps. "And I would hate for your whole family to come under investigation." She raises a sharp brow.

My eyes widen. "My family had nothing to do with anything."

She runs a hand over the top of her blonde hair. "It will take police and investigators months to come to that conclusion. Especially if I pushed." She lifts her chin. "How stressful it would be for everyone, including your father. I would hate to jeopardize his sobriety." She arches a brow. "Or you could come with us, and your family doesn't need to be investigated. The police might have questions for your family, but I can be very persuasive. I can assure the police will be understanding of your father's fragile state."

My mouth hangs open as I wonder what the fuck is wrong with her. Maybe having a bitch of a mother is the reason Aiden looks the way he does. The rumors about Nora Westling being a drug addict might have merit after all.

Her gaze drifts back to the window. "Do we have an understanding?"

"An understanding?"

She turns away from the view of the city to glide elegantly toward the door like this conversation is over. "Yes, you'll come home with us like Aiden and my husband want."

But not her. Maybe she never wanted to find Anna? "No deal. I'm not moving in. We can talk about weekend visits or something."

Her shoulders stiffen. "It would be a shame if your father was arrested."

My face flames with heat, and my hands ball into fists. It would be a shame if I kicked her ass out of the fucking window. "You can't have him arrested. He didn't do anything."

"Six months. Stay for six months and the police won't even question your father."

Her blank expression is gone. Her eyes are cold and hard. Her smooth face has been replaced with lines between her brows and around her eyes. I take a deep breath. "Two weeks and nobody in my family is questioned by police."

She laughs a manic sort of laugh that has me backing up a step. "Two weeks?" Her laughter dries up and her nostrils flare. "You have no idea what I'm capable of, little girl. If you knew, you wouldn't be testing me the way that you are."

Her eyes are wild, and I don't doubt she's capable of all kinds of crazy shit. I want to go back in time. I could have crashed at Grace's house on the day of the interview. Tilly would have been pissed but she would have gotten over it. Fuck Nick

Cabot for this. I pull at my lip ring, hating that I'm in this situation. "Three weeks," I mumble.

"That's not enough time," she snaps. "Two months and your father won't go to prison."

I study her face. She'd send an innocent man to prison? "Fine, two months. My dad has two months left anyway. And Tilly comes with me wherever I go."

"And you'll visit on weekends after that."

"After that, I'll visit one weekend a month for three months. Final offer."

She studies me and then she smiles, her face softening. "Fine. Glad we got that sorted out." She spins on her heels, leaving me to wonder what the fuck happened and if I made the right choice.

I follow behind her a second later, making it into the room as she's sitting down to take her husband's hand.

"She's nervous. This is a big change for Anna." She turns from John to Aiden. "Take Anna to collect her things. The plane will be ready to take us to the beach house in an hour." Her lips pull into a tight smile as she focuses on me.

Aiden bends down to kiss his mother on the cheek. "See you at the airport." He straightens and smiles at me. "Ready?"

Sighing, I move out into the hotel hallway where James is waiting. "Your mom is interesting."

Aiden's arm brushes against mine as we move into the elevator with James. "How so?"

"She threatened my family if I didn't come with you," I tell him, and he doesn't look surprised which has my eyes narrowing. Either he's used to this behavior or he thinks she was right in doing so.

"Mom's... she's struggled since you were taken. She sees a psychotherapist and takes a multitude of pills to function throughout the day and to sleep at night. She wants you home. She wouldn't actually hurt your family."

I shake my head because he's wrong. "It didn't seem like she wanted me. She made it seem like she was doing it for you and John, not herself."

"She has her moods, but she loves you. I'm sure she was just panicking about the thought of you not coming with us." He rubs the back of his neck. "I can talk to her if you want. If you don't want to come with us..."

My stomach flips as the elevator carries us down. Nora made it clear what she would do if I didn't agree to come. I'm not going to risk my dad being sent to prison. Nora has issues. Testing her wouldn't be worth it, and I can handle anything for two months. "I'll visit for a couple months like I said I would."

"I know it's going to take time for you to adjust, and things might be weird at first, but it'll be okay." He gives me a reassuring smile. The elevator door opens, and Aiden whispers, "I've missed you."

He doesn't look at me like he's afraid to see how

I'll react to his vulnerable words. Aiden Westling is nothing like the moody asshole I had pictured, and I don't want to hurt him. "I know," I reply, meeting his eyes and giving him a small smile. I really need to take that second test.

CHAPTER 11

James parks the SUV on the side of the street, and I hop out, leaving him and Aiden to wait. As soon as I open the door, the smell of garlic and cheese hits me. I kick my shoes off because the vacuum is sitting by the closet. Nana will throw a fit if she sees me walking through her house with my shoes on after she's done the floors.

"Is that you, Hayley? Come into the kitchen and eat," Nana calls.

I was already on my way. Nana can cook, and whatever she's making smells delicious. Nana's hovering over steaming pots on the stove when I walk in. The gray apron with pink trim Dad bought her is tied around her waist.

"Almost ready. Making spaghetti with home-made sauce. You hungry, baby?" Nana asks me over her shoulder.

I take a seat at the small table by the kitchen window. "Starving, Nana." I don't ask if she needs help because I know she won't let me. Cooking is a solo act for her. Tilly and I usually handle the dishes afterward.

I move the yellow curtains to the side and see the SUV is still parked on the curb. I wonder how long they'll wait before they think I'm not coming out? I'm going to take my time if this is my last day.

I'm not going to miss Nana. We were never close. Her and my grandpa traveled a lot before he died, so we only saw them a couple times a year. I just have this feeling like going with the Westlings isn't a good idea. I'm afraid to call Nora's bluff. I laugh lightly to myself. Look at that, something I'm scared of, a fucking princess.

I can handle two months. It's not like I'll be missing out on much.

Shit.

My job. I won't miss it, but I'll miss the income. I pull my phone from my pocket as Tilly's walking in.

"You're back. You weren't gone long." She drops down on the chair across from me. "Tell me everything."

With the phone to my ear, I hold my finger up to her. "Hey, Pete. Can I talk to Lisa?"

Pete transfers my call and then Lisa is on the other end. "Hello?" Her smoker's voice is deep, almost sounding like a man.

"Hey, Lisa, it's Hayley Thompson. Something unexpected came up, and I won't be back."

"You won't be back?"

"I won't be back to work. I wanted to let you know, so you could find someone to cover my shifts."

I wait for her reply but the silence on the other end has me pulling my phone from my ear. She hung up.

"You hungry, Tilly?" Nana asks, pulling a stack of plates down from the cabinet.

"Yes, ma'am," Tilly says and then taps her fingers on the table to get my attention. "You quit?"

"Yeah. Nora... convinced me to visit. You down? I'm not leaving without you."

She grins. "Yes! Of course I want to come with you."

I laugh lightly at her excitement. "We eat and then pack. I'll warn you Nora seems a bit nuts. I don't know how this is going to go, and it's temporary."

Nana sets full plates down in front of both Tilly and me. The steam from the spaghetti and fresh garlic cheese bread has my mouth watering.

"You girls mind putting the leftovers away? I'm meeting some friends to plan the bake sale at church."

"We've got it, Nana, but Tilly and I are going to stay with some friends out of town for the rest of the summer, so we won't be here when you get home."

Nana smiles. "That sounds nice. You girls have fun." She grabs her purse from the hook and then she's out the door.

"She probably won't even notice we're gone."

I laugh. "Probably not."

"So." She grins. "Tell me how it went."

"It was awkward. I still think this is weird. They have a five-year-old daughter and of course Aiden and Colt. Aiden and the little girl already think I'm their sister. Colt wasn't there."

"You are their sister. You have two brothers and another sister. I'll always be your favorite, right?" She rests her chin on her hand and bats her long eyelashes.

I roll my eyes and shove a mouthful of spaghetti into my mouth.

Tilly brushes her bangs from her eyes. "School starts in two weeks. Are we coming back for that?"

"Probably," I lie, not wanting to worry her. I'll think of something when the time comes.

We eat the rest of our food in silence. I glance out the window and see the SUV is still parked before Tilly and I get up to take care of the dishes and leftovers.

Once the kitchen is taken care of, we head to our room to the familiar task of packing. It doesn't take long since most of our things are at home. We brought the bare necessities with us here. I take a much-needed shower, change into a gray tank and black jeans, and then we're lugging our bags outside. The SUV is still parked by the curb. I was secretly hoping they would leave. Aiden and James hop out to help us shove our bags into the back.

Aiden nudges me. "We spend summers at our

Florida beach house. There's jet skis, a boat, a private beach, a pool, and a ton to do around town."

I nod, trying not to grimace. A beach vacation is the last type of vacation I'd take. Grinning, Tilly rushes into the back seat. I follow her, and Aiden and James move to the front.

"Buckle up," I remind my sister as the SUV pulls out onto the road.

"Mom and Dad are on their way to the summer home. Liv was getting tired and cranky, so they took the helicopter. We'll head to the airport now. It's only an hour or so by private plane."

"Private plane," I say. "I guess that's how we roll now, Tills."

"A private plane!" she squeals. "That's so cool! I'm going to call Margo from the plane. Oh my god, they are going to flip when I tell them you're Anna Westling!"

"No," Aiden and I say at the same time. We stare at each other, him with a lopsided grin and me with a raised brow.

Aiden twists in his seat to better see Tilly. "There will be a press release sometime in the next few days. Until then, nobody is supposed to say anything."

I pop my shoulder. "I'd be fine never saying anything."

"People would find out eventually," Aiden says.

"We probably need makeovers," Tilly says, grinning. "Just so we're appropriate to be in the spotlight. Highlights, manicures, facials, and new clothes, right, Hayley?" I give her a pointed look and her smile falls. "You're no fun."

Aiden laughs. "Mom is going to want to do exactly that."

"Is Nick going to be there?" Tilly asks. "And Casey?"

"Casey's in Hawaii with his family, but he'll be there soon, and Nick is on his way there now with my parents. Nick's cousin Rocco is staying with us too."

Tilly's jaw drops. "Rocco Cabot is going to be there?" She fans her face. "This is the best day of my life."

"Oh, someone you like more than Nick and Aiden?" I question and Aiden laughs.

"Rocco Cabot is the hottest guy alive." She inspects the clothes she's wearing and frowns. "I need to put my pink dress on before we get there."

"Mm." I nod, liking that idea. I want her to stay young and innocent for as long as possible.

"We're here," James says, shutting off the SUV. "Everyone ready?"

Hell fucking no, my mind screams, but I smile at Tilly and open my door.

CHAPTER 12

A little over two hours later, we're in front of a massive mansion. Yellow concrete seems to be never-ending. There are multiple levels, balconies, and windows. The word villa comes to mind even though I'm not exactly sure what that is.

Nora and John greet us on the patio as the sun is slipping behind the house. Liv's eyes are closed, her head resting on her father's shoulder. John supports her weight with one arm while pulling me in for a hug with the other. His shirt is soft against my face and smells like lavender and citrus.

Nora pulls Aiden to her side, brushing a lock of wavy hair from his eyes. Aiden's light blue shirt matches Nora's dress. They all seem to match with their pastel colors and crisp whites. A whole matching family and here I am in ripped jeans and a faded gray tank. My dark blue lip ring matches the bow in Liv's hair, so there's that.

Of course Tilly loves that they match. She even

looks like she belongs to them with her pastel pink dress and white headband.

John hugs me tighter. "I'm so happy to finally have you here," he says. "We all are." He pulls away and smiles at my sister. "You must be Tilly. It's a pleasure to meet you."

"Hello, Tilly. That dress is darling." Mrs. Westling turns to me with a tight smile I'm becoming all too familiar with. "I could have my personal shopper pick some things up for you if you'd like?"

Meaning, I hate your style. I've dealt with people like her, privileged and spoiled. I took a cleaning position last summer for a wealthy woman. These types of people are simple to deal with—nod, smile, and agree.

"Sure. If you want." She can buy me all the clothes she wants to, but it doesn't mean I have to wear them.

Nora smiles. "I'll give Claire a list. Come in and I'll show you around." She wraps her arm around my shoulders, steering me toward the front door.

"Come on, Tilly," I say over my shoulder, fighting the urge to shake away Nora's too tight grip. Nora leads us into a massive foyer, and I see yellow is the theme. We're shown two separate living rooms that are big enough to hold a hundred people each. Both rooms have gaudy chandeliers, stiff furniture, and maroon carpet. A two-story library at the center of the house is a room I can see myself spending time in. I bet it looks awesome at night because the ceiling is made of nothing but glass.

The maroon carpet and yellow walls continue to the second floor as well. The library is accessible from this floor too. There are two hallways with several bedrooms and bathrooms and a living room that matches the ones downstairs. Every corner of the upstairs has a large balcony overlooking something beautiful like the beach, a garden, or the pool.

Nora shows me where I'll be sleeping and then shows us Tilly's room a couple doors down. We head back downstairs and then Nora leads us through the kitchen to access the back door. The patio is covered, large, and decorated with furniture. She points out a private beach, boat dock, tennis court, and pool. Nora tells us this is a French-inspired home. I didn't know the French liked the color yellow this much.

By the time the tour is over, I feel like I've walked for miles. Even Tilly, who was the most excited about being here, has lost her pep and looks like she's ready to fall down.

"Thank you so much for showing us around and for letting me stay," Tilly says as we stop in the hall near the library. "You have such a beautiful home, Mrs. Westling."

Tilly is a good liar. The house is ugly and way too big. I don't see why they need sixteen bathrooms and thirteen bedrooms. Maybe famous people have their other famous friends sleep over regularly.

"Please, call me Nora." Her lips twitch. "Tilly is such an unusual name. Is it short for something?"

Tilly blushes. "It's short for Matilda."

"Oh, I see why you've shortened it. Tilly is a pretty name."

Not missing her dig, I narrow my eyes. "I think Matilda is a strong, beautiful name that suits Tilly's personality." I smile, tucking a strand of hair behind Tilly's ear. "Our mother loved it. It was her grandmother's middle name."

Tilly grins at me. "Mom said my name being Matilda felt like fate, like I was a gift from her grandmother."

Nora's smile is tight. "Of course, it's a pretty name." She gestures down the hall. "You girls look like you need to rest, so I'll leave you to it. Sara should have unpacked your belongings. Night."

I watch her walk away; glad she's finally gone.

"Can you believe we're here?" Tilly grins and then tilts her head. "Mrs. Westling kept calling you Anna. Should I?"

"Uh, definitely not. We'll let everyone else call me what they want, but my name is Hayley."

"Okay. Should we try and find our rooms?" She glances around, lowering her voice as she says, "I wonder where Rocco is?"

I lead us to the winding staircase. "I think you should have been Anna Westling. You fit in so much better here."

She giggles. "I do. Nora kept looking at your clothes in horror." Tilly's somber as we walk up the stairs. "She's your mom, Hayley. Your real mom."

"She *might* be my biological mom. Our mom was my real mom."

Peering over the edge, Tilly runs her hand along the metal handrail. "Still, this has to be freaking you out. This was supposed to be your life."

That's a punch to the gut. If Anna wouldn't have been kidnapped, she would have spent her summers here. I wonder what kind of person she'd be? If I had grown up here, would things be different for my parents and Tilly?

We move from wood and metal to thick maroon carpet. "This is it, right? Do you remember those paintings?" I motion to the large floral paintings lining either side of the hall.

"I think so. There were some of those downstairs too, though."

I chuckle under my breath. "I can't believe you told her she had a beautiful home."

"Um, it is beautiful. Did you see the artwork downstairs or the antique furniture?"

"Yeah, old, ugly, and dusty."

She laughs. "You're impossible." She points to a wooden door. "Maybe this?" She points to an identical door a few feet down. "Or maybe that?"

There are several closed doors in this hall. "This is bullshit," I hiss.

"I agree."

Tilly and I spin around to face the source of the deep voice. Nick Cabot stares back.

He tilts his head to the side, a frown on his face as he glares at my sister. "Why are you here?"

"Hayley wanted me to." Her eyes widen. "Wow, your photos don't do you justice."

His gaze moves up to mine. "Hayley, huh? I'm surprised you're not claiming the name. You moved in fast enough. What should I call you?"

"You can call me whatever you want."

He smirks. "Oh, I don't think you'd like that."

I narrow my eyes, not liking his tone. "We're trying to find our rooms. Can you help or maybe get Aiden for us?"

Nick steps closer, his chest almost touching mine, and then his arm shoots out, his fist knocking on the door behind me. Not taking his eyes off mine, he backs up, and then Tilly's scream has me spinning around. Rocco's in the now open doorway, grinning ear to ear. It's easy to tell him and Nick are related. They have the same hair color, same perfect skin, and the same nose. Rocco's eyes are hazel instead of brown, and he's half the size of his well-built cousin.

Aiden appears behind Rocco, eyes narrowed and glaring down at my sister. I slap my hand over her mouth for the second time this week.

Tilly quickly peels my hand away. "Holy shit! I can't believe I'm standing in front of you, breathing the same air as you." Her hands fly around dramatically. "You're Rocco Cabot! I've seen every movie you've been in."

Rocco chuckles. "It's nice to meet you... what

was your name?"

"Tilly. My name's Tilly."

"I see we have fans," Nick says from behind in a derogatory tone Tilly doesn't seem to catch.

"I am the biggest fan of all three of you. I've read everything and watched everything." She pauses. "But not like a stalkerish fan. Just a supportive fan. I'm sorry. I'm a little over excited. I've never met anyone famous and then today, I meet five of the most famous people." Tilly's eyes widen. "Six. Hayley, you're famous too."

Rocco's gaze moves to me. "Whoa, you do look like Aiden. Liv was so excited for you to get here. She kept saying Aiden's twin girl was coming." He laughs. "I think she passed out a little bit before you pulled up."

"Six famous people," Tilly mumbles. "I'm in the middle of history right here."

Nick crosses his arms. "What about you, Hayley Anna? Were you a fan too? Have any posters of us on your walls?"

My eyes widen slightly. I don't think I mentioned anything about falling asleep with my eyes on his poster. It's not like I wanted to. It was directly in front of me.

Tilly snorts. "No. She isn't a fan of anyone. I had to beg her to go to the interview."

Nick's eyes narrow like he doesn't like that answer. His gaze flicks to mine and then Aiden's.

"We're trying to find our rooms," I say to Aiden. "Can you help?"

Aiden chuckles. "Already lost? I see you have Dad's sense of direction."

That causes me to pause. At the word Dad, I instantly think of my dad, the one who adopted me. John Westling could be my biological dad. I might have inherited things from him like my crappy sense of direction. Or not. I'm still waiting for the lab to call and say there was a mix-up.

I give Aiden a tight smile as he leads Tilly and me to our rooms a hallway over from his. We tell Aiden goodnight and then Tilly and I move into her room. It's almost identical to mine—ugly as hell. The four-poster canopy bed is a dark wood that goes with the rest of the house. The comforter and canopy are floral. There's a cumbersome dresser with matching vanity, maroon carpet, and yellow walls.

We step out on to the private balcony. It's dark outside but the moon illuminates the water and beach. It's serene. I've never been to the beach or even cared to go. Now, I see what the allure is. At least at night. It could be a whole different story during the day. Walking along the beach at night would give me something to do when I can't sleep.

"Mom would have loved it here," Tilly says, leaning over the thick white rail. "She would have been so excited for you."

Not wanting to crush her spirit, I nod and smile. Mom might have been positive about a lot of things, but with this, I think she would have felt guilty. I can imagine her blaming herself for what the Westling family had to go through and for me missing out on my biological family.

Shit is going to hit the fan when the world finds out. I hope my dad will be sheltered from this in rehab. Maybe Tilly and I can convince him to stay there for a couple more months. I could beg Aunt Kathy for money to help me pay for it.

"Dad." I sigh. "We can't tell him about this. It could ruin his progress."

"I know," Tilly says. "It's too soon. But I think he'll be happy for you once the initial shock wears off." She glances over my shoulder and then focuses back on me. "Do you think Mom and Dad knew?"

"No way. They couldn't have. They were rule followers." I bite my lip. "Adopting me wasn't in their plan. They were a last resort to keep me with a foster family so I didn't end up in another group home."

"Remember Elfie," Tilly says, talking about the stuffed elephant that was our mom's when she was a kid.

I laugh. "Yes. It's the only thing that would calm me down. You gave it to me on my first day even though you hadn't slept without it since Mom and Dad adopted you." I eye her. "You okay sleeping here tonight?"

She grins. "Hell yes. I can't wait to get into that royal bed." She bounces over to her bags next to the dresser and pulls out pajamas.

"This whole day has been exhausting. Maybe I'll

actually sleep tonight. I'll leave my door cracked in case you need to come in."

"Thanks, but I think I'll be okay," Tilly says as she pulls on pajama shorts.

I slip into the hall and see John knocking on my bedroom door. "Hey, John. Need something?" Is it weird I feel weird calling him John? I don't want to call him Dad, but I bet he wants me to. I saw the way his mouth turned down slightly when I called him by his name.

He smiles. "I was coming to say goodnight. I'm catching a late flight to California. It's important Colt has a parent with him. I was spending the day in Florida when we got the call you'd been found." His eyes shine. "It still seems unreal but here you are." He stares at me for a moment, and then clears his throat. "Colt's filming tomorrow and then I'll bring him back here to see you. Unfortunately, he doesn't have long to stay. The set is making huge adjustments for him to come home. We can't exactly tell them we've found you, so I told them it was a family emergency."

"Okay. Sounds good," I say using my go-to line when I don't know what else to say.

"You going to be okay tonight? It must be weird not sleeping in your own bed. Is there anything you need?"

"I'll be fine. No worries. Goodnight." I force a smile onto my face. I find this whole thing awkward. I bet any other girl would jump right in and play the role of their daughter.

"Goodnight." John moves to the side, giving me access to my door. "Oh, An—Hayley. Let me give you my number in case you need to reach me."

He pulls out his phone, and I call off my number for him so he can text me his, and then I slip into my room, relieved he didn't try hugging me again. My mom was a hugger too, but she was my mom, so it's different. John is a stranger, even if we might share the same blood.

My room is a little bigger than Tilly's, and I have my own bathroom. I take a long shower before pulling on underwear and a sports bra. The bed is huge and hard. I thought the bed at my grandmother's house was bad, but this is worse. I slip under the scratchy floral blanket that has a weird smell, and then grab another pillow to shove under my head.

I lie awake in the dark listening to the quiet and expecting Tilly to tiptoe through the door. She only got used to sleeping alone a couple of years ago, and when she found out we were sharing a room at Nana's, she was happy. She doesn't like to be alone.

At the sound of my door opening, I roll over and sit up. "I was thinking we could bring your bed in here if you want, just until you're more comfortable." I stretch my arm toward the nightstand.

"That's so thoughtful of you," a deep baritone, who is not my sister, says.

CHAPTER 13

I click on the bedside lamp, and Nick struts up to the bed. He raises his brows as he takes in my chest. I want to roll my eyes. I'm sure he's seen plenty of women in their bras. Not that what I'm wearing is even a bra. It's a sports bra. Lots more coverage.

I lean over to scoop my shirt from the floor, and then I pull it on. My jeans are on the floor too, but the blanket covers my thighs. "What are you doing in here?"

"I see you're all settled in. Acting as if you belong," Nick says in a patronizing tone. "Couldn't get here fast enough, huh?"

"It's your fault I'm here. I didn't want this. You should have kept your mouth shut," I snap.

"You're the one who interviewed," he growls.

I cross my arms, angry he's right. If I'm going to blame him for this, I'd have to blame and be mad at Tilly too.

He leans in closer. "If you hurt Aiden, I will

bury you. Whatever you're planning, you better rethink it. In fact, I would suggest you drop this whole charade and leave."

I can't help but laugh. "What the fuck are you talking about?"

"Still playing games." He clicks his tongue while his eyes burn into mine. "You can keep denying you don't know anything, but I'll find out, and when I do, you'll wish you would have never come here."

I'm sick of threats. "Get the FUCK OUT of my room."

He does the opposite and steps closer. "I saw the way Nora was with you. She doesn't believe it either, does she?" His nostrils flare. "Should be proof right there when a mother knows someone is impersonating her daughter. She knew right away with the last girl too."

He's so close that I feel his breath on my lips. He's a predator, drawing you in with his good looks and sweet scent only to slit your throat. His gaze drops to my lips, and I lick mine. I think he might kiss me, but his arm darts out, grabbing my phone from the nightstand.

I can't believe I went all stupid for a second. If he would have tried to kiss me, I don't think I would have stopped him. "What the hell?" I lunge at him, trying to grab my phone back but he's too quick. I somehow end up flat on my back on top of the mattress with his body pinning mine. The fact he was able to get me into this position so easily has me pissed the hell off.

I shove his chest, almost pushing him off. He drops my phone to the mattress and grabs my wrists with his left hand to pin them above my head. His forearm comes down to my throat, and his knees move between my legs as I struggle to get free.

"Stay the fuck still."

"Fuck you!" I hiss but that's all I do because I can barely move. My whole body is heated, and I feel like snapping his neck. Using everything I have, I strain against him and then collapse, breathing heavily as he smirks down at me.

"Such dirty words for a princess." He wets his lips. "I thought you were a black belt in karate?"

"Fuck off."

Shifting to straddle my waist, he keeps my hands pinned above my head while removing his arm from my neck to grab my phone. He swipes across the screen, and I begin to buck, but all I end up doing is pushing my hips up between his legs, practically grinding against him. I still my hips but continue trying to get my arms free.

Concentrating on my phone, he tightens his grip on my wrists and squeezes my body between his legs. "You must really like dick," he says, not taking his gaze off the phone.

That has me pausing. *Does he think I like this?* I'm fucking pissed. My phone is personal, and he has no right to go through it. I might have been a little starstruck when I first met him, but anyone would have been.

He shoves the phone at my face, the bright light making me squint. He must be reading my text messages because he found one of the many dick pics Trent sent. I never saved them to my phone nor asked him to send them.

Nick brings the phone back to face him and swipes at the screen several times. "You only have ten contacts in your phone, and half of those are family members. Seems like someone can't get along with others."

I want to slap the smirk off his face.

He drops my phone to the bed. "James is digging into your past and everyone you know. Are you prepared to destroy this family when the lie comes out?"

"Why don't you think I'm Anna?" Maybe he knows something I don't.

His eyes burn into mine as he slides off of me and gets to his feet. "You have to have at least one memory." Crossing his arms, he takes a step back. "Tell me."

My throat constricts. I squeeze my eyes shut. If I'm Anna, one of my foster families were my blood and not the ones I'm told were. So many different faces bring up emotions that I don't want to resurface. My eyes snap open when I hear my door slam shut. Nick's gone, and I'm breathing heavily. I get up from the bed to push the lock into place only to swing it back open and march across the hall to Tilly's room. No way am I leaving my sister unprotected with a deranged lunatic living here.

***

When I wake up, Tilly's room is bathed in sunlight and I'm alone. I stagger out of bed, grabbing my phone from the dresser to see what time it is.

Fuck.

It's already noon. I'm sure Tilly's been up for hours and who knows what she's getting into. I swear if anyone fucks with her, I will kill them.

I have a hundred texts from my co-workers. Looks like Lisa announced I won't be back. I type out a text to Angie telling her I'm staying with family in Florida for a while. She'll pass the message to everyone else.

I move to my room to get dressed but my bags are empty. Nora had said something about someone putting mine and Tilly's things away, so I move into the closet. The walk-in closet is long and wide. Clothes hang on both sides, and there's a dresser against the back wall. Along the bottom left wall is a long rack filled with shoes I'd never willingly wear. Most of them either have heels or sparkly glitter covering them.

I bypass bright colors and frilly fucking things to where my clothes have been moved to the very back of the closet. I throw on my black New York tank and maroon skintight jeans and run my fingers through my hair as I head for the stairs.

Assuming Tilly might be in the kitchen, I head in that direction, but I don't remember exactly where it is and end up at a door that leads outside. I retrace my steps back to the stairs and try again. A minute later, I'm lost once more. I spin around, walk down the hall, and then take a right. I pass the library for the second time and end up in the foyer where a woman dressed in a maid's uniform is arranging a vase of flowers on a round table.

"Excuse me. Can you point me toward the kitchen? I'm lost."

"Yes, ma'am. Make a left out of here and then take a right at the end of the corridor. The kitchen will be halfway down on the left."

"Got it. Thanks."

"You're welcome." She goes back to arranging flowers and I make a left.

At the end of the hall, I make a right. That's what I was doing wrong. I kept making a left and that leads to a small patio near the pool. I make a left, and bingo. Aiden, Tilly, Rocco, and Nick are gathered around the kitchen island. Ugly wooden cabinets line every wall making the room feel smaller than what it is. The tile is a dirty yellow and the marble countertops are a mixture of color: cream, yellow, and brown. A mural of what looks like an Italian village is painted on the wall behind the double range.

Tilly's face lights up when she sees me. She abandons the pizza everyone is huddled around to skip over to me. "We're headed to the beach in a minute. I was going to wake you up after we ate. Come with me! I went down this morning and it's amazing. There are beautiful shells everywhere, and the water is perfect."

I love how her whole face is lit up. I want to snap a picture so I can always remember her like this. "I'll come for a bit."

She wraps her arms around me and then bounces back over to the boys to pick up her slice of pizza.

"Hey, An—Hayley," Aiden says. "Want some pizza?"

I glare at Nick as I brush past him to grab a piece of pizza, and then I shuffle back a few feet to lean against the sink. The large window behind me shows a nice view of the white sandy beach. I expect Nick to say something about last night or accuse me of some bullshit, but he's not even looking at me. I guess we're pretending he didn't threaten me last night.

"So, what are we supposed to call you?" Rocco asks me. "Tilly calls you Hayley, but Nora is calling you Anna, and Aiden..." He laughs. "Aiden seems confused."

"She wants us to call her princess," Nick says with a smirk.

I glare at him. "I'm not a princess."

"Technically you are," Aiden says.

"Told you," Tilly says with a satisfied smirk.

"What name do you feel most comfortable with?" Aiden asks.

I swallow the food in my mouth. "Hayley." I don't know why he'd ask. Hayley is the name I grew up with.

Aiden looks disappointed by my answer, so I look away from him. I eat my pizza while drowning out Rocco as he recounts a trip to Mexico that he took last week. I watch my sister hang on to his every word. Her hair and makeup are on point, and she's wearing the shorts she thinks makes her legs look long, therefore making her taller. Her red, crochet crop top leaves her shoulders bare, and her flat belly on display.

Rocco keeps throwing her little grins. She's too young to be starting anything with boys. I bite my lip. At least she's aiming high, I guess. Tilly is the type of girl that ends up marrying a doctor, lawyer, or businessman. I'll end up with a blue-collar boy, or alone, and there's nothing wrong with either.

When Rocco finishes his vacation story, Tilly grabs my wrist. "Come on. Let's go change."

I let her pull me out of the kitchen. On the second floor, we split up. I move into my closet and trade my jeans for frayed denim shorts, and then slip on slinky white sandals that are too fancy for my taste but the most casual beach shoe out of the others.

While I wait for Tilly, I flick through the clothes seeing at least a quarter of them aren't half bad. I guess in a weird way this could be Nora's way of showing affection. To possibly mend whatever is going through Nora's head, I pull off my shirt and bra and slip one of the new shirts on. It's a tight and silky cheetah print crop top. It's not my style but I know Tilly will like it because of the Prada tag.

"Ready?" Tilly chimes, from the closet door. "No way. She already filled your closet?" Tilly pushes past me to search the goods and then begins to excitedly shout off brand names I've never heard of.

I lean against the doorframe. "Tills, are we going to the beach or are we playing dress up?"

Laughing, she hangs a shirt back up that she was admiring. "Beach now, dress up later."

Making our way to the beach, Tilly recounts every detail of her morning. It sounds like everyone has been nice to her, even Nick.

Deciding to walk barefoot in the white sand, I slip my shoes off on the patio. The sky is light blue and cloud-free. It's one of those perfect days people gush about. Rocco and Aiden are already in the water tossing a ball back and forth, and Tilly quickly removes her clothes to join them. Her hot pink bikini shows off her slim body.

"Come on, Hayley," she calls over her shoulder before catching the ball Aiden tosses her way.

"I'm gonna chill here and watch," I say, dropping down to the warm sand and relaxing back on my forearms. I watch the three of them toss the ball back and forth until they decide to pull out skimboards. Rocco is too hands-on as he shows Tilly how to ride the little waves.

An unexpected body dropping down next to

me has me shifting to the side. Using my hand to shield my eyes from the sun, I stare at the newcomer as his gaze skates over my face. He's wearing dark blue swim shorts and nothing else. His upper body is thick muscle. A thin line of hair runs from below his belly button to disappear beneath his shorts. Dammit, this guy is a twenty on a scale of one to ten. Even better than his pictures.

He smirks. "You look like him." He laughs. "Is it creepy I think you're hot?"

I snort. "What?"

He shakes his head, and his wavy auburn hair falls into his eyes. He pushes the pieces away, green eyes shining. "I'm Casey, Aiden's friend."

I nod. "I know who you are. I have the internet." I can't remember what his family is famous for, but I do remember his name—Casey Brooks. I almost wish I paid attention to celebrity gossip, so I knew more about him.

"Why aren't you out there?" He nods to the water.

I shrug. "Not feeling it."

He chuckles. "What? Fun?"

I narrow my eyes and then focus on the water. I've never been eager to let people in. Spending time like that leads to connection and then attachment. People aren't permanent, but the feelings they leave behind are. I'm not so worried about myself. I've been burned too many times to give in to this temporary situation. I can tell Aiden's already getting attached and so is John.

The more distance I put between them and myself, the easier it will be for them when I leave.

"Not very talkative, huh?" His gaze drifts back toward the water. "Who's the chick?"

"My sister."

With a cocky grin, he turns his whole body to face me. "Oh, yeah?"

"She's only fifteen, so hands off."

Casey's gaze moves over my shoulder. "Yo, Nick!" Grinning, he gets to his feet, brushing sand from his shorts with one hand while waving Nick over with the other.

They both hover above me, and I don't like feeling like a sitting duck, so I hop up. Nick is just as built as Casey if not more so. His shorts are black, and his smooth skin is tan. His pecs and abs are fully defined as are the muscles in his arms. His chest glistens in the sun from sweat or maybe baby oil. He looks so fucking solid, like his muscles have been replaced with sculpted stone.

His eyes meet mine, and he smirks. I pick my mouth up and turn to focus back on the water. I grind my teeth, mad at not schooling my emotions better. I was practically drooling.

"Casey!" Aiden hollers as he jogs toward us. "You made it."

Casey grins, hugging Aiden when he makes it to us. Rocco and Tilly stay behind in the water, wrapped up in their own little world. Laughing, Tilly falls off the skimboard, and Rocco hauls her up from the water by her waist, keeping a hold of her a little longer than what seems necessary.

Aiden plants himself next to me, draping his arm around my shoulders. The water from his arm drips down my back, helping to cool down my heated skin.

I turn away from the water to smack Aiden's stomach which is all hard abs. "I saw you dunk my sister."

He laughs. "She sent a wave at my face. I had to get her back."

I laugh and shake my head.

"Nick, tell me this isn't freaky as hell," Casey says, waving toward me. "They look so alike."

Nick's eyes narrow, and his nostrils flare but he doesn't say anything. It looks like Dominick Cabot hasn't shared his feelings about me with his friends. That's interesting.

"We do look alike. It's pretty fucking cool. When I first saw her, I just knew," Aiden says.

He's grinning so wide that I can't help but smile. He seems proud to be my brother. He could have taken one look at me and been a preppy prickly dick. My stomach flip flops because if I'm not Anna, I think he will be the most upset out of his family.

"She's a hotter badass version of you, bro. You need to step up your game. Maybe get some tattoos or something."

I forgot the shirt I'm wearing shows off part of my tattoo. Aiden's gaze follows Casey's to my torso. His eyes widen as he takes in the ink there.

"My mom would lose her shit if I got one." Smiling down at me, Aiden rolls his eyes. "If you haven't noticed our mom's big on appearances."

"Oh, I've noticed. I've got a whole closet full of girly outfits from her." I hold up my phone. "And she messaged me about a hair and makeup appointment."

I can't help but to discreetly admire Nick's body again. Are all insanely rich people drop-dead gorgeous? If I'm Anna, why don't I look perfect too? I'm not ugly but I'm not a knockout either. It must be the expensive things they had growing up, like organic food and beauty creams or whatever.

Nick catches me staring at him and narrows his eyes. "She's got to get the royal princess ready for her debut. What did you expect, Your Highness?" Aiden and Casey laugh like he's joking, but he's being a dick.

"I guess the queen will find out the princess isn't some little doll she can play with," I say, smiling sweetly at Nick.

"Nora's a princess, not a queen," Casey says and then laughs. "I always forget that, dude. You guys are royalty. Weird I get more chicks than you, Aiden. Your royal dick must not be that great."

"Casey, man, shut the fuck up. My sister," Aiden says, his arm dropping away from me to shove Casey's shoulder.

A laugh bubbles out at how red Aiden's cheeks turn. "I'm all grown up, Aiden. I know boys and girls have sex."

Casey throws his head back and laughs.

"I bet Hayley Anna knows all about sex, right? You look like the type."

I open my mouth to tell him off, but Aiden steps up to him, and says, "Dude, what the fuck, Nick? You can't talk to my sister like that."

"She looks like you, but so do hundreds of other girls. I think you should do a second test. This is too big not to be a hundred percent sure. It happened before."

Here we go. Let out how you really feel, Nicky. He might be a dick to me, but I can respect he's being real with it and looking out for his friend. I might not like him, but I'd expect the same from Grace if I were in Aiden's shoes.

"This is completely different, and you know it," Aiden says.

"I think a second DNA test is a good idea. Like I told you before, I'm not convinced. Something could have happened at the lab. Hell, maybe even do a couple more tests. And run my sister's sample too."

All three guys stare at me with confused expressions, but Aiden's face morphs into disappointment.

"Why your sister's?" Casey asks.

"Like a placebo. It would probably be best to surprise the lab with multiple anonymous samples. Secretly slip mine in and see what happens."

"You don't think you're his sister? You don't believe you're Anna?" Casey asks, brows dipping low.

I shrug, my gaze darting between all three. "I just want to be sure. It's all a little crazy."

"I assumed you had memories. You don't remember?" Casey asks. "Nick and Aiden remember you."

My gaze shoots to Nick and then Aiden. Could the memory I have of one of my foster brothers be Aiden? That doesn't make sense. I thought the foster family that screwed me up was after running away from the people the cops said were my biological parents.

"I've had a few foster brothers, but..." I bite my lip. "The earliest one I remember is Dean." My brows furrow as I concentrate on the memory. "I was on a bike, my foster dad running behind me. I crashed into a parked car. I could hear Dean crying and that made me cry even though I wasn't hurt."

"That was me, Hayley. You called me Dean. And that was Nick's dad's car you ran into. I remember it. See, I told you, you were Anna." His smile is so wide and eyes beaming.

"It could be a coincidence," I say, my voice a tiny whisper. "Lots of kids wreck on their bikes."

"What's another memory?" Nick asks, his intense gaze boring into mine.

I stare at the sand, shuffling through the past in my head. The memories of Dean hurt the worst even if there are only a few. I remember loving him so much and then he wasn't there anymore. "I remember Dean reading me my favorite book. I think we were the same age, but he learned to read before me, or maybe he had the book memorized. I had to help him turn the pages because they kept sticking—"

"Goodnight Moon," Aiden whispers.

Swallowing a lump in my throat, I look up at him and nod. "I loved that book. I remember the paper moon hanging next to my bed." I glance at Nick and suddenly those dark eyes are almost familiar. If I were to take away his strong jawline and add chubby cheeks, it could be him. He could be the other boy I have hazy memories of.

"Holy shit," Casey breathes. "I don't think you need any more tests."

"That's not enough to prove anything," I say.

"What's going on?" Tilly asks, suddenly appearing next to me.

Rocco jogs up, slipping into the circle we've all seemed to form. I back away, feeling like I'm being weighed down.

"You okay?" Casey asks, stepping forward.

My gaze darts to Aiden and then to Tilly. "I need a minute."

I speed walk to the house with my heart hammering against my chest and my throat dry and scratchy. I thought Dean was a boy from a foster home. I remember his mom floating around the kitchen in her long dress while Dean and I watched her make a cake. I can't picture her face, but I remember how I felt—I loved her. It broke me when they were no longer around, just like other families I bonded to.

If the people I'm told were my biological parents aren't, and I'm Anna, they could be the people who kidnapped her—me. I remember the evil woman's pointy witch nose and her blood-red nails that dug into my skin when she yelled at me.

I make it to my room and flop down on the bed, hugging my pillow to my chest, I let a couple of tears slip-free. Rarely do I feel this emotion—sadness. Usually, I rage. Right now, I feel lost and vulnerable. I don't like unpredictability and that's my life right now.

In the back of my mind, the lab was going to call and say they made a mistake. Tilly and I would be back at Nana's in time for her to start her sophomore year of high school. If I am Anna, these people won't want to let me go. I've never been the selfless type. I will ultimately do what's best for me and staying with the Westlings isn't it.

My mind starts to drift to the what-ifs, and that's dangerous territory. I don't want to spiral.

I dry up the tears, but my brain is threatening to drive me insane, so I grab my phone and head to the bathroom. Turning the volume up all the way on my heavy metal playlist, I step into the hot spray. I drop my head, letting the powerful jet of water pound against my neck and shoulders. The music helps to block out my thoughts, and the hot water helps to ease the tension from my muscles. After a couple of minutes, I robotically wash my hair and body.

Wrapped in a towel, I step out of the shower

stall and head to the closet to dress, but I stop outside the bathroom door when I see Nick sitting on the edge of my bed.

His gaze slowly drifts over my body then up to meet my eyes. "You should keep your door locked. Someone had a reason to take you before. They could try again."

I quirk a brow. "Oh, now you think I'm Anna?"

He lifts a shoulder. "Don't you? Only Anna could have those memories."

I study his face. "Maybe, but I still want to do a second test." I bite my lip. "Aiden said there weren't any leads in the case?"

Nick tilts his head to the side in thought. "John said it had to be someone they knew because of how quick it happened. The house was guarded and secured. From the time the security system went down to when Nora called the police, only five minutes had passed. They had to know the layout of the estate and that Nora was the only adult home. Everyone they knew was questioned. John hired private investigators and threw money at everyone. Nora's family hired people too. But from what I've been told, there were never any real suspects. Do you remember being taken?"

I shake my head.

"Do you remember me?" Nick whispers so low I'm not sure I hear him.

Clutching my towel, I inch closer. "What?"

Shaking his head, he gets to his feet. "Nothing." He walks past me. "Keep your door locked."

I watch him leave the room. *I do remember you, Nick*, my mind whispers. He's the one who made me the moon.

CHAPTER 14

The shrill alarm coming from my phone makes me want to throw it across the room. I almost hit snooze, but my shrink back home said a routine is essential for insomnia. I'm starting to wonder if maybe my internal clock isn't up to par with the rest of society. I sleep great after four a.m. but not a minute before.

I shoot a text to Tilly telling her I have a headache. That's code for going to stay in bed all day. I arrange the pillows so I'm propped up and pull up the Netflix app on my phone. I haven't had a chill day in forever.

Episode after episode blur together. I'm completely zoned out. I love it. A knock at the door forces me to hit pause. I grab my shirt from the floor, slip it over my head, and run my fingers through my hair. I open the door a crack.

"You okay?" Aiden asks, straining to better see me. "Tilly said you were sick."

"It's a headache. I'll be fine. Gonna chill in bed

today."

"Okay. Let me know if you need anything."

"K. Thanks." I push the door closed and make my way back to bed. I'm taking the whole day off. I wish I could fast forward the next two months.

***

My alarm goes off at nine like usual, but this time, I feel rested and less like smashing my phone to pieces. The Netflix binge and day in bed helped. I shuffle around my room getting ready and then head to Tilly's room.

I swing the door open and of course, it's empty. Her ass likes to get up at the crack of dawn and have a full day before I get up at nine. I make my way toward the stairs, but the sound of crying stops me before I reach them. I peek into the upstairs living room and find Nick with Liv on his lap. They're sitting on one of the many cream-colored sofas in the room. Liv's head is resting on Nick's shoulder, her arms tucked tight against her chest, and Nick is rubbing her back. His large frame has her looking like a toddler.

A girl who looks to be a few years older than me is standing next to Nick. She spots me and blushes. Her shoulder-length hair falling into her face as she leans down to whisper something to Nick. Her plain gray dress, like the maids, reaches her knees and hides any figure she might have.

Nick's hand stills on Liv's back as he notices me. I feel my cheeks heating up as we stare at each other. I better not be fucking blushing.

"I'm sorry, Miss. Is her noise bothering you? I can take her to her room."

I give the girl in the old lady dress a funny look because what the fuck, and then I focus back on Nick, telling my stupid cheeks to cool it. "What's wrong with Liv?"

"Anna!" Liv says, pulling her head from Nick's shoulder to look at him. "Maybe Mommy will wake up for her?" She brushes untamed hair from her tear-stained face and then shifts on Nick's lap to see me better.

"Why don't you go with Sophia, and I'll check on Mommy? Don't you want to find some seashells?" Nick asks her.

"No!" Liv whines, dragging out the word into a howl. Fresh tears spill from her eyes and trail over her round cheeks. "I want Mommy. She promised to make muffins with me today."

I frown, not understanding what's going on, but her tears are squeezing my heart. Growing up in the system, I regularly witnessed kids crying with no one to comfort them. "You want to make muffins, Liv? Tilly is the best at making muffins. I bet we could talk her into helping us."

Peeking up at me, she wipes her nose, smearing green snot across her face.

"We could add fruit to them. I love strawberry and blueberry muffins the best," I say, trying not to grimace. That's a lot of snot.

Liv smiles. "I like blueberry muffins too."

"Do you want to help me find Tilly, so we can make some?"

She nods her head and scoots off Nick's lap.

"Why don't I help you clean your face and change out of your pajamas before you help," Sophia says, reaching her hand out to Liv.

She takes Sophia's hand and looks over to me. "Wait for me, okay?"

"I'll wait here," I say, and a toothy grin spreads across her face before she bounces away with who I'm assuming is the nanny.

"What was that about?" I ask Nick.

He runs a hand through his hair. "Nora's doc adjusted her medication again. She's been spending most days in bed, and Liv is missing her."

"So, is the adjusting of medicine and her not getting out of bed to take care of her child something that happens often?"

Nick gets to his feet. "Don't be so quick to judge her. She lost her daughter, and it broke her."

"Then why have another kid?"

He sighs. "I think she was trying to fill the hole of losing Anna. Before John hired Sophia, Aiden, Casey, and I took care of Liv when John had to be with Colt on set. It's been a fucking mess. We all thought Nora would get better if we found you." He shrugs. "Maybe she's too damaged."

I hate that her kids suffer because of her actions, but a part of me is pulling for her to overcome whatever she's battling because I don't like the term "damaged." I was deemed damaged, but with love and therapy, I'm a functioning adult. I might still have some issues, but I haven't been to prison. Isn't that the key to passing enough for society's standard?

"I remember the moon you cut out for me," I say. "At least I think it was you. I remember a boy with dark eyes, shaggy brown hair, and dirty fingernails. The few memories I have of him, he was playing in dirt with little metal cars." I grimace, remembering how gross I thought he was at the time, always covered in dirt. "The boy lost my moon book. I remember being so angry, but then, he made me a moon cut out and helped me hang it next to my bed." I don't know why I blurted out the memory, but I don't regret saying it. "Was that you?"

Nick nods, his eyes wide. "Yeah, that was me." He clears his throat. "I can't believe you remember that. Fuck. I didn't think we'd find you but Aiden... he was so persistent about the interviews. I have a lot of memories of you."

"You do?"

"I was six when you were taken. I guess being older, I remember more." He rubs the back of his neck. "I sorta ruined your moon book. Do you remember that?"

"Ready?" Liv says, bouncing over to me wearing a pink sundress. Pulling at her pigtails, she eyes my hair. "I have long hair like you." She takes my hand.

I let her lead me to the door when I'd rather stay

and talk to Nick. I want to hear his memories. I glance over my shoulder and see him watching me walk away. The usual scowl on his face is gone. He looks happy. And dammit if it doesn't make him look even sexier.

***

Two hours, a big fucking mess, and twenty-four muffins later, I've decided I never want to have kids. Liv is cute but I'm already exhausted. She hasn't stopped talking or moving, and she almost died twice.

"How's it go—holy shit." Casey steps up to the island, taking in the scene.

Every space on the kitchen island is occupied with muffin trays, measuring cups, spoons, egg-shells, and flour. Flour has managed to get over every surface in the kitchen, including us.

"What the hell?" Casey lifts his hand, gooey egg white dripping from his palm. "Yuck."

"Language, Casey. You said shit and hell," Liv says as she picks apart a muffin and shoves a piece into her mouth.

Tilly laughs as she places batter-covered bowls into the dishwasher.

I toss Casey a dishrag so he can wipe his hand, and then I drop to a bar stool. "FYI, I can't ever be left alone with Liv. She almost died."

Casey laughs. "What?"

"She almost died *twice*. Hayley tripped and al-most pushed Liv into the open oven," Tilly says, trying not to laugh. "And then she almost stabbed her with a knife." This time she does laugh, and Casey joins her. "Hayley sucks in the kitchen." Tilly turns to me. "That's why Mom banned you. Remember the banana bread incident?"

"Mommy didn't ban her," Liv says around a mouthful of food.

Tilly frowns, and I don't know if it's because she misses Mom or she's just now realizing we don't have the same mom anymore, and our lives are forever changed. Or maybe I'm projecting. My shrink said I tend to project my feelings onto other people.

"That's right, Liv. Your mom didn't say that," I say, getting up and glaring at the mess. I swipe two rags from the drawer and toss one to Casey. "Why don't you make yourself useful."

Kids, plus hours of cooking, are exhausting, but with the help of Casey, Tilly and I get the kitchen back to what it was before muffins. Casey takes Liv to find Sophia, and Tilly and I head upstairs to clean ourselves up. I change into hunter green lounge pants and a white shirt and then shuffle out the door.

I push Tilly's door open, but her room is empty and so is her balcony. She didn't even tell me what she was going to do. I close her door behind me and catch Aiden and Nick in the hall by my door. "Hey, know where Tilly is?"

"She and Rocco were headed to the beach. She's determined to master the wakeboard," Aiden says.

I frown, not liking the idea of Tilly and Rocco alone together or how comfortable Tilly has become here in only a couple of days.

Reading my face, Nick says, "He's harmless. Rocco's a good kid."

I raise a brow. "He's a boy. A teenage boy." I'm not only worried about Rocco, I'm worried about everything as a whole. Tilly is here having the time of her life. She assumes these people are permanent because they might be my blood, but she should know better than anyone blood doesn't mean shit. Tilly's biological mother was a horrible woman who hung onto her parental rights for longer than she should have been allowed. At least our mom got her right away. Tilly didn't have to bounce around different homes making and breaking friendships.

"Nick's right, Rocco won't hurt her. They're just friends anyway." Aiden clears his throat. "I wanted to show you something in my room."

"Okay," I say, eyeing him. "Show me what?"

He gestures for me to follow, and I do, with Nick following behind. Aiden's room decor matches mine, but the size of his room is a lot bigger. A lounge area with a sofa and two chairs makes up a small living room when you first walk in. Inside a large archway, a huge bed is against the far wall near French doors. It doesn't look like he's added any personal touches to the room. Maybe rich people don't do that with vacation homes.

Aiden gestures for me to have a seat on the sofa. I drop down, and he moves over to a desk near the French doors. The desk is small, and the top is bare besides a small metal lamp and a laptop computer. I eye his room again. It doesn't look lived in. The bed is made, nothing is on the floor, the dresser top is empty, and there's nothing on the walls besides a few ugly paintings.

"Scoot to the middle. It'll make it easier."

I do what Aiden says and he and Nick drop down on either side of me. Aiden passes me a small photo album he pulled from the desk. The brown leather is worn, and the album is only an inch or so thick.

"This is the only one here. There are more in California," Aiden says.

On the first page is a picture of a small girl and boy. They're both smiling wide, rows of baby teeth on full display. The little girl is wearing a frilly red dress, white tights, and black shoes. The little boy has on a red shirt and black slacks. I run my finger over the girl's eyes. They look like my eyes.

I turn the page and see a picture of two babies sitting on a white blanket in the grass. The boy is dressed in a frilly blue one-piece with a silver rattle in his hand, and the girl is in an equally frilly pink outfit. Her face is tilted up at the sky, the light shining on her face. Her eyes are closed, and her lips are pulled up into a soft smile.

The next page is a picture of John. He has a small

child in each arm. The little girl is pouting, and the boy looks mad. He looks an awful lot like the Dean in my hazy memories.

"That was taken a few weeks before you were taken," Aiden says. "We were almost four. You were taken a week before our birthday."

"When's your birthday?" I ask, not looking up from the page.

"March tenth. It must be weird finding out you're not the age you thought you were."

I grunt in response because yep, weird as hell. I can't take my eyes off the photo. There is no denying this girl and I looked similar as children. The earliest photo I've seen of myself was when I was almost six and my hair was short and blonde. Put short blonde hair on the girl in the picture in front of me and they could be twins. But don't all children look similar? "I had blonde hair, not brown," I say, feeling some kind of emotion about saying it out loud. I think I don't want to disappoint Aiden.

"I know. James said whoever took you dyed and cut it," Aiden says with absolute certainty. "The investigators assumed that would happen, so it's not a surprise."

I turn the page. The little girl, Aiden as a little boy, a lady I don't recognize, and a little boy who can only be Nick, are standing in a driveway next to a garage door. Child Nick's arms are crossed, and he wears a deep scowl much like he does in all the photos I've seen of him online. His dark eyes are angry as he glares at the little girl. The woman holds his hand, but he isn't holding hers back.

The little girl's eyes are red, her face is wet with tears, and her mouth is wide open in what looks like a frustrated cry. Even though all the children look unhappy, the picture makes me smile. Candid photos are rare amongst the Westlings, and in all of their media pictures they are always looking their best. These children all have messy hair, disheveled clothes, and both Aiden and Nick are barefoot.

"That's my mom," Nick says. "Her and Nora were best friends. They met each other at boarding school in New York when they were ten."

My nose wrinkles at the thought of boarding school. "I guess it explains why she doesn't have an accent. How long were Nora and your mom there?"

"They graduated together, so until they were eighteen."

Aiden laughs. "I forgot this picture was in here." Aiden points at a picture of young Nick with something brown dripping down his shirt and arms. "Dad said you dumped chocolate sauce on Nick because he broke your favorite Barbie doll."

Aiden turns the page and points out some of our cousins. He flips through a few more pages, and I notice a theme. "Does your dad not have a lot of family?"

"His mom died when he was a kid, and his dad was never around. He was raised by his grandmother, but she died a few years ago. Dad has a few half brothers and sisters, but he didn't grow up with them."

"Does he not talk to them then?"

"I think he used to but not anymore."

The last photo is of Nora in a hospital bed with a tiny baby in each arm. Grinning from ear to ear, she's staring up at the camera. She's almost unrecognizable from today's version of herself.

"She doesn't smile like that anymore," Aiden says.

"I've noticed. Does she still talk to your mom, Nick?" He's been mostly quiet this whole time, but I've felt his eyes on me, taking in my reaction to the pictures. And his right leg is pressed against my left, something that's been making my stupid stomach flutter.

"Not really. My mom tries, but Nora..."

"Knock knock. Hey, guys, look who's here."

John's in the doorway with Colt Westling by his side. Besides the dirty blond hair, he looks exactly like John, but I already knew that. Colt is in all the movies and shows girls Tilly's age like to watch. I think Colt and Rocco starred in a TV series together. Tilly is going to lose it when she sees him.

I bet Nora would be proud of the way Colt is dressed. He's the poster boy for preppy. Aiden is too, but Aiden's hard face and clipped words lose him points with the media. Colt Westling is the boy next door, and everyone loves him. He's been on every talk show I can think of while Aiden hasn't been on any.

"Hey," Colt says, stepping farther into the room and looking me over. An amused smile splits his face. "I bet Mom's freaking out. Are those piercings real?"

I laugh and John playfully swats the back of Colt's head before taking a seat on one of the chairs across from the couch.

"Yep, real, and I have a tattoo."

Colt's eyes widen. "No way. How'd you get a tattoo?"

I chuckle. "I walked into a tattoo shop."

He nods approvingly. "That's so cool."

"Maybe don't tell Nora about the tattoo." John smiles. "She's..."

"Complicated," I say, filling in the word for him.

John's smile is weak as he nods his head.

"I have so many questions," Colt says, dropping down to the chair next to John. "Did you always know you were Anna? Is your family freaking out?" He frowns, looking at John. "Isn't it sad we didn't find her sooner. All this time she was with another family."

John's gaze meets mine, and I see so much sadness there. "She's here now," John says. "That's what matters."

"Because Aiden pushed to do the interviews. Mom fought him like crazy. I bet she feels bad now," Colt says, crossing his arms.

I guess Colt doesn't have the compassion toward Nora Aiden seems to have. Colt's demeanor completely changed when he mentioned his mom. I eye Aiden. "She didn't want you to do the interviews?"

"She... Mom thought the worst when the kidnappers stopped contacting them about ransom," Aiden says.

Everyone is quiet for a second before Colt asks me, "What's your favorite food?"

"Eh... I don't know. I guess if I had to pick one, I'd say alfredo."

"Chicken or shrimp?"

"Chicken," I say. "I'm not a fan of seafood."

"Aiden too." Colt grins, leaning forward. "Beach or city?"

I see where this is going. "Neither. I like the mountains," I say.

Colt laughs. "Aiden too. Zoo or aquarium?"

"Again, neither. I think it's fucked up to cage animals unless it's a rehabilitation center."

Colt's lips twitch like he's fighting a smile. "They're safer in captivity."

"So," I say, not able to hide the attitude slipping out. "That's not any excuse to enslave a living creature. Live free or die."

Colt, Nick, and Aiden all laugh while I glare.

"I've said the exact same thing," Aiden says, pulling in his smile. "I know what it's like to be caged. You don't truly get to experience living."

"Chocolate or vanilla?" John asks, seemingly amused by the twenty questions going on.

"Chocolate, but mint chip is my favorite." I glance to the side meeting Aiden's amused stare.

He chuckles. "Same."

I don't want any of them confusing me and Aiden's similarities to mean I fit into their little family. I don't and I won't. Plus, I don't plan on giving up my life and family back home to get to know a new one. I'm riding out the time I was forced to agree to. I open my mouth to tell John what Nora said to me back at the hotel, but I decide not to. I bet he couldn't stop her from doing what she threatened.

John stands, stretching his arms above his head. "Hey, guys, why don't we head down to the beach for a bit?"

Everyone agrees and John leaves the room to get Liv, but I'm still feeling some type of way about the questions I was asked.

"If you won a million dollars, what would you do with it?" I ask Aiden.

He frowns. "I... I don't know."

"Dude, what about that Aston Martin," Colt says.

Aiden nods. "Yeah, maybe."

"I'd pay off my mother's medical debt so my father wouldn't be burdened by it. Then I'd pay for him to go to a better treatment center. After that, I'd pay for college for me and my sister," I say, not having to put any thought into my answer. "What did you do for your tenth birthday?"

He sighs, not meeting my eyes. "I had a circus-themed party."

"I was doing a mandatory seventy-two-hour

hold. My foster mother at the time was mad I wouldn't clean the room I shared with two other girls. They were the ones that made the mess. My foster mom told the hospital I was out of control and needed to be evaluated." I watch his eyes turn hard, and it makes me feel better because I don't want him thinking now that I'm here life is peachy keen. "What was your first job?"

"I get it," Aiden says.

I don't think he does.

"We grew up differently. I know that," Aiden says. "My life wasn't bad, but it wasn't perfect. And I know being here is probably hard for you. Just because you didn't grow up here doesn't mean you don't belong."

Because I'm never one to hold back, I wave my hand in front of myself. "Look at me, Aiden. I don't fit in."

Colt laughs. "You're a reflection of Aiden's true self. You think he's this preppy boy and he's not. He hates to disappoint Mom."

Damn. I totally get that. Luckily, my mom wanted me to be myself. Even still, I would sometimes do things I didn't want to because I knew it made her happy. I wouldn't sacrifice myself to please her but that's because sacrificing myself wouldn't have pleased her. I can't imagine what it would have been like to have Nora as a mother growing up.

"You're judging us without getting to know us," Aiden says.

I nod. "Yeah, a little, but it's not just that—"

"There you guys are," Casey says, walking into the room and smiling wide. "John said it's beach time." He winks at me and then drops down in the empty chair.

"You guys ready?" John asks, poking his head into the room.

Liv skips past him and stops next to the couch. She's wearing a purple one-piece with a pink mesh wrap over it. Her hair is in a bun, and she's hugging a doll to her chest. She is so freaking adorable but dangerous. She pulls you in with her cuteness to suck out all your energy and leave your brain a mushy mess. Even still, you can't help but get attached to her.

She smiles. "You wanna build sandcastles with me, Hayley?"

I want to go to my room and be alone, but I say, "Sure, Liv." I force a smile, trying to trick my brain into being happy and that this tiny human isn't a little scary

CHAPTER 15

Colt Westling is a lot like Tilly, and of course, they hit it off right away. Turns out they are only fifteen days apart in age and begin talking joint birthday details as they follow everyone to the water, leaving John, Liv, and I to hang out on the sidelines and build sandcastles.

After a couple of hours swimming, Rocco and Colt run to grab supplies from the house to build a giant sandcastle. I never knew there was special equipment for it. Buckets and shovels are brought down to the beach, and by the time the sun has begun to set, we have a sandcastle as tall as Tilly.

Sara, one of the maids, walks down to tell us Nora wants us up for dinner, so we abandon our castle and move inside to clean up for dinner.

After changing clothes, I make it into the massive dining room after everyone else. I've never seen a table so big. Even with all of us sitting down, there are several open chairs. I'm between Tilly and Aiden. Nick's next to Aiden and holding his attention, and Rocco's next to Tilly and holding hers, so I have time to observe. Nora seems zoned out. She smiles when spoken to but besides muttering a few words occasionally, she's quiet.

I feel sorry for Liv who is trying so hard to get her mother's attention. John and Colt are good about distracting her, but I see Liv's hurt.

After dinner, I head upstairs while everyone else heads to the informal living room to watch a movie. I'm wiped out from the sun and all the human interaction, but it was nice seeing Tilly so happy. If she hated it here, we'd be gone.

I lie back in bed, my brain going over the events of today when there's a knock at the door before it's pushed open. I reach to grab my shirt from the floor, but it's not there. I think I left it in the bathroom, but whatever. The sports bra covers enough.

"I thought I told you to lock this?" Nick jiggles the handle and examines it. "It's not broken."

Only an hour has passed since dinner, so the movie can't be over, yet here's Nick in my room. He's wearing the gray sweats he wore to dinner but the white shirt he was wearing has been replaced by a black muscle shirt that reveals how fit his upper body is.

Staring at my torso, he tilts his head to the side. "Why'd you pick a compass?" He moves forward, stopping at the side of my bed.

He looks different when his eyes aren't narrowed in hate and his upper lip isn't hooked into a constant snarl. Like Aiden's public photos, Nick's are dark and ominous. The world would lose their shit if they saw this human version of him. Long gone is the bad boy who will break your heart, and instead, is a guy you could see a future with. Dominick Cabot is beautiful, and he's in my room, probably checking on me.

Thoughts of him taking me from behind have my cheeks heating up. I bet he's a hair puller. I know he can be rough and fierce. My scalp prickles at the thought of his hand wrapped around my hair while our sweaty bodies move together. Yep. It's officially been too long for me.

Nick frowns, his eyebrows narrowing. Oh, shit. He asked me a question, and my horny ass totally spaced out. Compass. Tattoo! I raise up on my elbows, staring down at black winding lines that make up the intricate compass on the right side of my torso. A dangerous-looking dragon is placed at the center of the compass. "I picked a compass because it reminds me that I'll stay true to myself no matter what comes my way."

"And the dragon?"

Sitting up all the way, I laugh. "I just thought it looked badass. You got any tats?"

"Not yet. I haven't found anything that calls to me." He pulls a small joint from behind his ear. "You looked stressed at dinner. Do you partake?"

Grinning, I scoot over. "Um, hell ya I do. My shrink actually suggested it to help with sleep."

Nick takes the spot on the bed I just vacated

and leans against the headboard. My stomach flutters with excitement. *Calm the hell down*, I silently scold myself. *He's here with a peace offering, not to fuck your brains out, you slut.*

"Shrink?"

I clear my throat. "Someone I started seeing after my mom passed. My dad was losing it and I wanted to. I had to think about Tilly, so I got help." I laugh lightly even though a lump is forming in my throat. "It's ironic. For years, my mom had been trying to persuade me to see a shrink. It took her death for me to finally do it."

"I can't imagine losing my mom." He lights up and passes it to me.

"I hope you don't have to for a very long time. I take it your mom is nothing like Nora?" I take a hit and hold it in before blowing out a cloud of smoke. In a house this size, you don't have to worry about anyone smelling the aroma of illegal activities. The smoke will probably never even reach the bedroom door.

"No, she's nothing like Nora, but you have to remember Nora wasn't always the way she is."

We smoke the rest in silence. Nick moves to the bathroom to toss the roach into the toilet, and I fall back on the bed, staring up at the painted angels, flowers, and clouds on the ceiling.

"It's pretty," Nick says.

I roll my head to the side to see he's lying next to me, staring up at the ceiling too.

"I wonder who painted it?" is the last thing I

remember saying before I'm waking up in a pool of drool. Lifting my head off the pillow, I wipe my mouth with the back of my hand and force my eyes open. The room is fully lit from the sun and stinging my eyes. *What the fuck?* I've never slept like that. I didn't wake once.

I'm on top of the cover, sprawled out on my stomach, and Nick is asleep next to me, our legs tangled together. He's on his back, his mouth slightly parted, and his chest rising and falling peacefully. He's fully dressed, and I'm in my sports bra and shorts, so we obviously didn't mess around. A few days ago, Nick had written me off as his enemy, and now... I would almost say he considers me a friend, but I'm not here to make those.

"Nick," I say through a rough and scratchy voice as I untangle our legs and flip onto my back. "Get up." I nudge him with my foot, but he doesn't budge, so I do it a little harder.

"Fuck," he grinds out, lifting his head from the pillow.

Not only does a little drool shine on the right side of his mouth, but his eyes are bloodshot, and his hair is sticking straight up on one side.

I fight back a smile. "You look like shit." He looks rough as hell, but he's still hot as fuck.

He studies me and laughs. "I can imagine if I look anything like you, sleeping beauty."

I laugh lightly. "Shut up." I rub the sleep away from my eyes and sit up. "What the fuck kinda weed was that?"

Nick runs a hand down his mouth. "Some new shit I got from Casey. I didn't realize it was going to knock me on my ass."

I yawn and stretch. "You got any left? I haven't slept that good in a long time."

"Back in my room." Nick cracks his neck. "Fuck, your bed sucks." He runs his tongue over his teeth and combs his hair down with his hand. "I need water and a shower."

I climb over Nick's legs to get off the bed and grab my phone from the nightstand. I check my messages while trying to flatten down my bed-head. I have a new one from Grace, so I shoot her a quick reply telling her I'm visiting family in Florida. I'll need to let her know what's really up soon. "I'll get some from you later." I stretch again, my back popping a little. "Damn I even feel good."

"I feel hungover. I think I got too much sleep," Nick says, dragging himself to the door. "Catch you later, sleeping beauty."

He swings the door open, and Casey's there with his hand up, ready to knock. Casey's eyes widen and then he laughs. I groan. This doesn't look good. The last thing I need is everyone here thinking I slept with Nick. I'm not saying I wouldn't, but it wouldn't be done publicly.

"You're already fucking?" Casey laughs again. "Aiden's going to kick your ass."

"Shut up, Casey." He pushes him back a step. "That weed you gave me knocked us out last night. What the hell was that shit?"

160

Casey peers over Nick's shoulder taking in my room, me, and the bed. "So, you two slept together, literally? Well, that's boring." He dodges another shove from Nick and then slips into my room. "Nora sent me up to tell you you're needed downstairs."

"Great," I mumble.

"I feel left out," Casey says. "Tonight's my turn. We can get smoked out and talk about the meaning of life and shit."

I laugh lightly. "Sure, Casey, as long as you supply the weed, I'm down."

"Come on. Let her get ready," Nick says, walking out the door and pausing in the hallway.

Smiling wide, Casey stares at me a minute, and then he winks, backs out of the room, and shuts the door behind him.

Running my fingers through my tangled hair, I move into the closet. I pull on my shredded at the knees gray jeans and a sleeveless lavender shirt from Nora's side that I would never normally wear. See, I'm making an effort to wear the clothes she wants me to. I'll never go full Westling but a little here and there won't kill me. I switch out my blue lip ring for a purple one to match the shirt.

The house is quiet as I walk through it. Back home, our house was never quiet. If talking or laughing didn't fill the house, music or a TV did. The only time I ever remember it being quiet was when I got home from hanging out with Grace to find out my mother had been rushed to the hospital after a car accident.

My shoulders slump in disappointment as I step into the kitchen. I was hoping to run into my sister who isn't messaging me back, but instead, Nora's icy glare meets mine. She's dressed in a teal formal dress, and her hair is pulled into a tight bun. Neither of us speak or move. Her eyes flick down to my clothes and she frowns. She opens her mouth but closes it as Aiden walks in with Liv and Sophia.

"Mommy! Hayley and I made muffins yesterday. Do you want to try one?" Liv bounces over to Nora's side.

"You'll call her Anna, not Hayley," Nora snaps and Liv's face twists, her smile slipping away.

I take a deep breath, so I don't yell. "Nora, Liv probably heard everyone else calling me—"

"Mom!" Nora snaps, nostrils flaring. "Or mother is how you'll address me, young lady."

I narrow my eyes. I won't call her that, but I don't need to voice it in front of Liv who looks like she's about to cry. Does she not see she's hurting her child? She wanted me here to please her family, so she has to have a heart somewhere in that stone chest of hers. Liv backs away from Nora to huddle next to Sophia.

"I heard about the *muffins*." Nora practically growls the word. "Martin mentioned his supplies were missing. That could have been a disaster had guests been coming over."

"Mom, we don't have guests over anymore, not

to this house anyway," Aiden says. "And Hay—they didn't know to ask Martin first."

Nora's face softens the tiniest bit, but then she looks at me and her scowl returns. I think back to the picture of Nora in the hospital bed. Light radiated off her in that picture. This woman in front of me is rigid and cold. Her face is tight, and her lips are pulled into a thin line.

Nora Westling is beautiful in the beautiful villain type of way, like Maleficent or Black Widow. I haven't run into many people that scare me. Nora's unpredictability combined with her power and never-ending supply of money scares me.

"Anna, Claire's in the main room setting up her things to do your hair. I've told her you're a family friend."

"Got it," I say, crossing my arms.

With her chin held high, she clicks her way out of the room on her heels, and Aiden begins listing breakfast choices for Liv instead of addressing the elephant in the room—Nora doesn't like me.

***

Two hours later, my hair has been trimmed, layered, and glossed. It has never been so straight or shiny. My eyebrows have a higher arch, my nails are polished, and my face has been painted and contoured. I feel different—fake. I don't like it, and I hope Nora doesn't expect me to keep this up. I like my hair when it's wild and wavy. It's easier to throw up into a messy bun that way. My eyebrows make me look alert, almost like I'm surprised, and I don't know how Claire did it, but my nose looks smaller. Not that it was too big to start with. This isn't me. I didn't sign up to change myself.

Nora's standing in front of me, a scowl on her face as her gaze runs over me. "The makeup is fine, but why didn't Claire apply your nails?"

Nora's gaze snaps to the petite blonde woman who changed my look. Claire looks like she's going to throw up.

I rub my thumb over my smooth nails. "I didn't need them. I already have nails, and she buffed them." I hold up my hand. "See, good as new."

Nora's frown deepens. "They were supposed to be longer and painted silver."

I don't tell Nora I think painting the tips of your fingers is weird. Nail polish wigs me out. "I think they look fine."

She hands Claire a silky silver dress. "Put this in her room, and make sure she has shoes to match." Claire hurries away, and Nora glares at me. "Go with Claire. If the dress doesn't fit, let her know. I'll figure out the nails later."

I bite my cheek because I don't wear dresses, and I have never worn or wanted to wear heels. "I understand your image of Anna isn't me. I'm sure I'd be very different if I'd grown up here," I say, trying to show empathy. "The way things turned out isn't your fault, but I need you to understand that I have boundaries," I say, being true to myself, something I will always be. "I don't do dresses or heels, but I'm willing to wear the clothes in the closet." I throw in a smile even though she looks pissed. Who the fuck wears fancy dresses around the house?

"Why are you being so difficult?" she hisses. "My Anna wouldn't be like this. If you're going to take her place, you will play the part."

I narrow my eyes. "You're the one who threatened me into coming here. I didn't sign up for this shit, and I never said I *was* Anna. That was the test that I'd be more than happy to retake."

Her eyes flash with rage. "You'll watch that tone and language, young lady."

She glares at me, and I silently begin listing off the things in the room so I don't go off on her ass.

"A reporter will be here in two hours. I will not allow you to wear that" —she eyes my outfit— "on national television."

I put my hand up. "Hold up. National television? Why do *I* need to be on television? Can't someone snap a picture of me?"

"A picture? You can't be serious. Anna Westling's homecoming is going to be on every news station around the world. There's a prepared speech and approved questions you'll answer."

Oh hell no. "That is not happening. I'll take a picture. I'll even put the dress on for the picture, but I am not going on television to repeat some speech or answer questions. I haven't even called my family to tell them. I need to do that now, I guess. It would've been nice if I had been given a heads-up about this."

Nora's naturally pale face turns bright red and then tears spill from her eyes. "My sweet Anna wouldn't speak to me like that! You're here to punish me, you awful girl!" She flies from the room, leaving me with one thought.

This bitch is crazy.

CHAPTER 16

"I know. It's unbelievable," I repeat, agreeing with my aunt Kathy. I've given her a run-down of what's transpired since the interview and asked her to spread the news to everyone except Dad.

Aunt Kathy is the one who keeps in touch with all the distant family members. Mom and Dad both have small families. Mom had her sister Kathy, Kathy's kids, and her mom. Her mother, who I only knew from getting the occasional birthday or Christmas card, lives far away and is in poor health. Dad has his mom, recluse brother, and a couple of his cousins we'd see on the occasional Thanksgiving. Dad's dad died a few years ago, leaving Nana a widow.

"I'll call rehab and see what to do about your dad. I don't think they have news and stuff there, so he probably won't find out."

I rub my forehead. "I hope not. Keep me posted. I'll talk to you later, Aunt Kathy."

"No problem. Call me if you need anything, Hayley. I mean it."

"I will. Thanks." I end the call as Colt and John walk into the sitting room I'm in. I waited here thinking Nora might come back and want to rationally talk things out.

Liv runs in grinning. "Daddy and Colt are going to the airport, and guess what, Hayley?" She bounces up and down.

"You got a new toothbrush," I say with faux excitement.

Her little face scrunches up. "No."

"Hm." I tap my chin. "They're going to ride a spaceship."

Liv laughs. "No, silly. I get to go! Daddy said I can come to the set." She bounces over to John and hugs his legs.

John chuckles, running a palm over the top of Liv's head. "Why don't you see if Sophia needs help packing. Colt, you mind helping Liv? I want to talk to Ann—Hayley for a second."

"I got this," Colt says, taking Liv's hand. "Let's make sure you get all your favorite stuffed animals ready to go."

"Yes!" Liv shouts. She bounces her way out the door while listing off names of what I'm assuming are stuffed animals.

John sits down on the other side of the sofa. "We haven't had much time to talk. How are you doing?"

I twist to better see him. "I don't know yet. I'll

get back to you on that."

He chuckles. "Fair enough. I wanted to talk to you about school. Aiden and Casey are starting freshman year next week. I'm sure I can pull some strings to get you in if that's something you're interested in? I know they'd both love for you to be there."

"Oh..." College has been my goal for a year but not in California. "I don't think it's the right time. What about my sister, though? She's going into tenth grade. Is her coming to California and enrolling into school there going to be a problem?"

"No, of course not. She could do that, or we hired a tutor through an agency for Colt. That's another option for her. She's your sister. She will always be welcome." He chuckles. "Plus, Colt has claimed her as his sister too. He thinks it's awesome they are so close in age."

Hearing that stirs up different emotions. I should be happy Tilly is fitting in with my... in with the people who might be my family. It could be easy for me too if I let it. It's tempting to cave and accept this new life. I could see myself having a relationship with everyone but Nora. My dad, though. Just because he's out of sight doesn't mean we forgot him. Tilly knows that, right? He'll want us home when he gets out.

"Hayley?" John asks, snapping me out of my thoughts.

"Uh, thank you. I'll talk to her and see what she wants to do."

"Let me know, and I'll make arrangements. I better make sure everyone is ready to go. I'll see you back in California in a few days." He stands, and so do I. "I'd invite you along, but then Aiden would want to come, and Nora would..." He struggles to find the right word. "It's better this way. You'll have plenty of time to visit the set and spend time with Colt. Our home isn't far from where Colt's filming or from where Aiden's going to be staying at school."

I nod. I don't have anything to say to that. I would rather be going back to Tennessee. Voicing that thought wouldn't be productive. It would hurt John, and I don't want to do that unnecessarily.

John heads for the stairs and I head outside to find Tilly. I don't see why Nora wants me in California. She doesn't like me, Aiden will be in school, and John and Colt will be filming. That'll leave Liv and the nanny. Whatever. I'll use the opportunity to find a job in Cali and save money for school and a car.

I'm closing the back door when Tilly, Rocco, and some guy their age, walk up the patio steps. The boys don't notice me, but Tilly does.

"Whoa. You look amazing. I hope I'm next for the makeover."

I wave my hand in front of my face almost forgetting about the makeup. "Don't get used to this. I'm never doing it again."

The back door opens and John walks out with

Liv in his arms. Sophia is a few steps behind, carrying two small pink suitcases and Colt has his arms full of stuffed animals.

"John?" Nora's high-pitched voice comes from inside the house and then she's storming onto the patio. "There you are." Her gaze darts to the bags in Sophia's hands and then back to John. "You're leaving now?" Her eyes turn hard. "I spoke with my family. They'll be here Saturday. You have to be here."

John's brows shoot into his hairline. "That's in two days. I thought they were coming to California next week?"

"They didn't want to wait. They insisted, and you know how they are." She straightens the collar on his gray polo. "I need you here."

He adjusts Liv in his arms. "I'm sorry, Nora, but I can't. You'll be okay."

Nora smiles stiffly, her eyes darting to everyone and then back to John. "I need to speak with you inside." Her voice is a sharp hiss.

Setting Liv down next to Sophia, he sighs but doesn't protest as he follows behind his psychotic wife. I want to slap Nora. Liv was smiling wide when John walked out the door with her and now her face is blank. Nora didn't even acknowledge her.

"Come on, Liv. Let's go to the car and wait for Daddy," Sophia says, ushering her in the direction of the attached garage at the side of the house.

At least I think that way leads to the side of the

house where the wrap-around driveway meets the garage. This house is ginormous. I need a map.

"I'm out," Colt says, meeting my eyes. "I'd suggest you do the same. Mom is going to be batshit crazy for the next couple days."

"Why?" Tilly and I ask at the same time.

"Nora's family hates her," Rocco says from the patio chair he's lounging in. "Everyone knows that."

"No, they hate Dad," Colt says. "That's why they're mad at Mom. They didn't want her to marry him." He brushes a lock of hair from his eye and grins. "Oh, they are going to flip over the piercings. Maybe I should see about staying longer." A loud bang comes from inside, and Colt's smile disappears. "Scratch that. Good luck. Might want to find the best hiding places in the house or spend a lot of time outside."

"Don't scare her. Nora's family isn't that bad," Rocco hollers at Colt's back as Colt speeds away. "I spent a few summers with Aiden and Nick at your cousin's house. Your family isn't that bad, and I'm sure they'll be nice to you. You're the long-lost princess."

Tilly lifts a strand of my hair. "You look like a princess now, minus the piercings."

I brush her hand away. I don't even know what to think. I've never been the type to try and impress people. Maybe something good can come out of this. They'll see I'm not princess material and tell Nora to kick me out before the press is alerted to my presence. I could always act as unprincess-like as possible—speed the process along.

"Why are you smiling?" Tilly asks. "What are you thinking?"

I tug my sister to my side. "That I love you so much." I kiss the top of her head as she's breaking free from me.

She laughs. "Liar." She pushes her damp hair from her face. "What's Nora's family going to think about me?"

I lift her chin and wink. "Naturally, they'll love you just like everyone else you meet does. Your Tilly charm will pull them in, and they'll think you have to be Anna instead of me."

Tilly giggles and I grin. "In your dreams, Hayley."

"So, she's Anna?"

We all turn our attention to the kid sitting next to Rocco, realizing we fucked up. His hazel eyes are wide and his mouth partly open.

"Shit," Rocco hisses. "Dude, Logan, you can't say anything."

Logan runs a hand over his short brown hair and mumbles, "Yeah, I won't."

"Colt?" John says, hurrying out the door looking frantic.

If the woman's husband can't stand to be around her, what does that say? From what I hear, John's never home, and from what I'm seeing, it's probably true.

"At the car," Rocco tells him, and John doesn't waste any time sprinting down the patio steps, throwing a goodbye over his shoulder.

Nora rushes onto the patio a second later shouting "coward" in the direction John went. Her gaze slices to me, pure hatred burning in her eyes. "You. Will. Wear. That. Dress." She spins around and marches inside, screaming for Sara to meet her in the formal room.

"What the fuck?" I mumble. Everyone's family has a little crazy, but the rich and famous might take the cake, or maybe it's just this family

CHAPTER 17

"Nora is totally wigging out," Rocco says, moving through the door Nora left open after she stormed through it.

"She seems to do that a lot," I mumble as I follow behind him.

Tilly turns around and shakes her head, her way of scolding me.

Two maids are gathering colorful bowls filled with food and setting them onto a metal rolling cart. The smell of taco seasoning fills the room making my stomach growl.

One of the maids rolls the cart out the patio door while the other tells us the patio table will be ready shortly. I may be minimalistic, but having a personal chef cook your meals would be amazing. Mom was the cook, and once she died, we went from home-cooked meals to soggy, frozen dinners. Working full time, doing everyone's laundry, keeping the house clean, and trying to keep Dad from drinking himself to death didn't leave me time to cook.

Nick walks in and my stomach switches from growling from hunger to fluttering with excitement. My mind flashes to the first night when he had me pinned against Danny's door. A part of me wants to fuck with him to see if he'll do it again. That's the fucked-up side of me, the side my shrink wanted me to work on before pursuing another relationship.

But I never said anything about a relationship. Nick could help relieve my tension and stress in the best way. Everyone talks about teenage boys and their hormones, but they don't talk about how teenage girls have them too. We get just as horny and think about sex just as much as guys.

Nick pulls a bottle of water from the fridge and pauses with it at his mouth. His eyes are wide with surprise as he stares at me. Setting the bottle down without taking a drink, he licks his bottom lip and then smiles. His attention causes my stomach to squirm. How he makes simple tan shorts and a gray cotton shirt look sexy as hell, I don't know. Maybe it's the way he fills them out or the dominant aura he omits.

He steps next to me, and then whispers, "I see Nora got a hold of you."

"Unfortunately," I say, trying to sound in control of my lusty emotions.

He flicks a strand of my hair. "Leave it to Nora to try changing something that was already beautiful," he says so only I hear. Looking past me to Rocco, he takes a sip of water and then leans back against the kitchen island. "What the hell has gotten into Nora? She was screaming at one of the maids."

I feel my cheeks turning red from his comment, and I'm glad he's not focused on me to see.

"The royals are coming in two days," Rocco says. "Nora's flipping out." He gestures to the friend at his side. "There's a party at Logan's. We were talking about heading over soon to avoid the house."

"Party started about an hour ago, and will be going all night," Logan says. "Come whenever you guys want."

"I can't wait," Tilly says, grinning.

Some sisters might try to stop their siblings from partying, but not me. Tilly has a good head on her shoulders. She's been to parties and had alcohol. She doesn't get carried away. I'm more worried about the boy next to her. Rocco drops his arm around her shoulders and whispers something to her like it's the most natural thing in the world, and it probably is for him.

Tilly isn't some groupie he can take advantage of. My sister is way too innocent. The way she's looking at him while he talks party plans with Logan makes me want to kick him out and lock her away.

"Let's eat first. I'm starving," Rocco says, his fingers purposely brushing against Tilly's arm in a soothing way that makes me want to rip them off.

I move my eyes to my feet as I follow them outside where the maids are laying out everything needed to make tacos. It's weird seeing my baby sister, who has never cared about boys, cuddled up to one. Rocco holds out a chair for Tilly and then scoots his so he's pressed up against her. Eating will be a nice distraction from watching my sister getting groped by a famous little shit.

"Chill, mama bear," Nick whispers in my ear, his warm chest pressing against my side. "Rocco won't hurt her."

I tilt my head to get a better view of Nick. "She's too young."

"How old were you?"

"I was her age, but I wasn't as naive about relationships as her. Our mom kinda exaggerated love." I lean my back against a pillar on the patio and face Nick.

"Oh yeah? How so?"

I laugh. "That fairy tales are real. That we'd find our prince charming and live happily ever after. I don't want her heart to get broken."

"I'm guessing you haven't been in love with that bleak outlook of yours."

I bite my lip, thinking about my ex Toby. We'd probably still be together if he hadn't gone to jail over a probation violation. He was the closest thing I've had to love, but it wasn't love. My shrink made sure to drill that into my head. "What about you? I haven't seen any women in the tabloids. Are you a good little virgin, Nicky?"

His laugh is deep. "Nope, and I don't need to ask you about your status." He grins. "You don't get hips like that from sitting still." Smirking, he tips the water bottle up to his mouth.

I arch a brow. "Oh yeah? You like what you see, Nicky?" And then I realize I'm flirting, and I look away. I don't need to complicate things further by starting something with Dominick Cabot, even if that something is no-strings-attached sex. I need to change the subject. "Where's Aiden?"

"Him and Casey went to Miller's."

"What's a Miller?"

"Oh shit." His eyes widen, his head turning to the patio table. "Nobody called you Anna, did they?"

I follow his gaze to Logan. "He knows, but said he isn't going to tell anyone."

Nick rubs his chin. "Fuck. He better not. Miller is Logan's brother. He came over to invite us to his party. Aiden's walking Miller home, didn't want him hanging around. Miller would blab his fucking mouth to everyone if he found out. We told Miller Aiden's cousins were visiting from Oregon when he saw Tilly at the beach with Rocco. If word got out before Nora says it's time, we would all pay. She can be a control freak." Nick chuckles, but I'm a little scared if I'm being honest.

I have more to lose. I need to do whatever I can to stay under her radar. She's the type to be on one of those shows where women snap and murder everyone around them. "I'm going to have a chat with Logan and make sure he keeps his mouth shut." Nick laughs and follows behind me.

My stomach growls, demanding I give it a taco before lecturing Logan. "Food first," I mumble. I set two tortillas onto a plate and then load everything on them. I see queso cheese and tortilla chips, so I add that to my plate too. I grab the chair across from Tilly since both the ones next to her are taken by Rocco and Logan.

Nick drops down on my right with a full plate. I feel the dark and dangerous energy he emits. It's distracting, making me want to focus on him instead of my food. I think I feel his eyes on me, but when I look up at him, he's focused on his plate. I grab my taco, and my eyes close as salt, lime, and spice hit my tongue.

I finish a taco in three bites and then point at Logan while dipping a chip into warm queso. "You. My name is Hayley, and I'm Aiden's cousin. I'll break your fingers if you tell anyone different. Got it?"

He hides his smile into his glass, and I lean forward, arching a brow.

"She isn't joking," Tilly says. "I've seen her break fingers before."

Logan moves his gaze to Rocco like he would know if I'm joking or not.

"I wouldn't cross her," Nick says seriously. "She's broken more than fingers."

Logan's smile disappears and he swallows. "Got it."

I chew and swallow the chip. "And you'd know that how?" I ask, twisting to face Nick and lowering my voice so only he can hear.

"James has a file on you."

"Right." I take a bite of the other taco on my plate. Everything in those files is probably negative shit like fights, suspensions, and arrests. I know my reasons for the things I did, but what were his? What caused Nick Cabot to be so angry, and how did he learn to reign it in? Or maybe he's learned how to cover up his crimes.

I make two more tacos while Rocco and Logan talk about the upcoming party like it's a magical trip to Disney World. Rocco makes sure Tilly's included in their conversation, and I do appreciate that. She's such a social butterfly. I finish off both tacos and then start on the chips and queso.

"Or maybe I was wrong and that's where you got your hips," Nick says, his eyes shining as he hands me a napkin.

I wink, using my tongue to clean my lips instead. "You were right the first time." Fuck, I just flirted again. *What the fuck is wrong with me?* It felt completely natural to do. I get to my feet. "Tilly, we should go get ready."

She jumps up, full of excitement, and Rocco's gaze moves to her legs and ass.

"We'll meet you guys at the party." I glare at Rocco and then Logan. "Remember what I said."

Nick stands. "It's hard to take you seriously when you've got—" He runs his finger over the corner of my lip and then licks his finger. "Taco sauce on your face."

I'm not a blusher but I blush and then giggle. I rarely do that either. Still giggling like an idiot, I grab Tilly's arm and pull her into the house with me.

"Did Nick Cabot really just do that? Is there something going on between you and him?" Tilly asks, sounding way too happy.

"There's nothing going on. But there is definitely something going on with you and Rocco."

A gorgeous smile lights up her sun-kissed face. "I like him. We clicked right away. It's effortless and fun, just like Mom said it would be."

I pull her to a stop at the bottom of the stairs. "Lust feels like that. It doesn't mean he's your prince charming. You're fifteen."

Her smile falls, and she crosses her arms. "I'll be sixteen next month, and Mom and Dad met when they were teenagers."

"Mom was nineteen and Dad was twenty."

"Age doesn't matter, Hayley. It's the souls." She marches up the stairs.

She has it bad. "Be careful and take things slow. He's famous and has everything that comes with it."

"He's famous but that doesn't mean he's a bad person."

"Just be careful." I open my bedroom door. "Come on. I think Nora thinks I'm a couple sizes smaller than I am."

Clapping her hands and smiling, she bounces into my closet. I grab my brush from the top of the dresser and run it through my glossy hair, forgetting for a moment I was made over today. Whatever Claire put in my hair must prevent it from tangling. I toss the brush back and give Tilly my attention as she creates a one-woman fashion show.

Aiden texts to see if we're ready, and I tell him not yet and we'll meet them there.

"You know you'll never be a real model, shorty," I say as she struts around my room in a baby blue romper. I grin at her glare. "Just keeping you humble."

"Shut up. You're like three inches taller than me, and I don't want to be a model but if I did, I would." She strikes a pose. "So, the romper for the win?"

"Four inches, and definitely. It matches your eyes." I glance at the clock on the dresser. "You ready? I think we should take Colt's advice and get outta here."

Tilly shakes her head. "You need to get ready."

"Right." I move into the bathroom and wet a rag. I scrub the makeup away until my face is red and blotchy. Tilly walks in as I'm swiping black liner under my eyes. "Almost done." I fluff my hair up with my fingers adding the volume back to it Claire glossed away.

"You didn't have to wipe off the makeup," she says, resting her hand on her hip and following me back into the bedroom.

"I'm laying low. I'm Aiden's uncool cousin from Oregon."

"You can't lay low if you stand out." She moves into the closet and out of my sight. "Trust me, big sister, I've got you. I know your style." She comes out with clothes and sets them on the bed. "This will help you blend in."

I eye the fabric she picked out. Nothing is pink, so that's a plus. I slip on a lacy, cream-colored crop top that fits snug against my skin. Dark jean shorts and gold flip-flops are next. I inspect myself in the mirror. "Fine. I don't hate it." I grab the black quarter sleeve button-up from the bed and slip that on, leaving it unbuttoned.

Tilly holds up a thick boho style bracelet. I roll my eyes but slip it on. "Maybe you'll be a fashion designer since you can't be a model," I tease.

She fiddles with the drawstrings on her outfit. "I would love to be a fashion designer."

"Yeah? I can see it. You'd be good."

She smiles and brushes her long bangs from her face. "Duh. Okay, makeup and then I'll be ready."

I lie on my stomach in bed while watching Tilly take her time with mascara and eyeliner. She really is beautiful. I know I tease her about not being able to be a model because she's so short, but she could. Her face is perfectly symmetrical, and her eyes are the most beautiful shade of blue I've ever seen. Her eyes pull you in while her personality keeps you there.

She runs gloss over her naturally pink and plump lips. "Done." She smiles at me over her shoulder. "We both look fantastic."

I pick my head up from the palm of my hand. "I wish I had as much energy as you." I grab my vibrating phone and check the text from Aiden. "They're on their way to the party. He said Nick's mad we didn't want to walk with them." I laugh and send him a text telling him we'll be on our way soon. "Wanna take a nap first?" I ask Tilly, jokingly.

"Grab an energy drink from the fridge. You aren't going to want to miss this. How are you not more excited? Were you even listening to Logan?"

"Not really," I confess. "You know I'm low-key when it comes to parties. A small group of people, a fire, and beer is all I need. I'm mostly going for you, but you'll be up Rocco's ass forgetting I'm even there."

She laughs. "Maybe. At least walk me over and see if the party is as great as they made it out to be."

I head for the door. "A bunch of rich kids bragging about their money, I bet it sucks."

CHAPTER 18

I was wrong. The party is nothing like I expected it was going to be. Hundreds of tiki torches line a winding path to the front lawn where a two-story house with sharp angles and countless windows sits. It's far enough off the main road that the other houses aren't visible. The porch is small in comparison to the rest of the house but still big enough to fit the live freaking band.

If the band wasn't enough, off to the left side of the lawn, two men are driving the crowd around them wild by twirling flaming batons and blowing fire from their mouths up into the darkening sky.

"This is insane!" Tilly shouts over the music. "Aren't you glad you came?"

"This was worth seeing!" I agree, my mind trying to take everything in. Barely dressed men and women carry silver trays filled with colorful drinks as they weave through the bodies of people. "Let's find Rocco! Did he text back?"

"I forgot to check!" Tilly swipes at her phone screen. "Yep! He said he's in back by the pool! That was twenty minutes ago. Hope he's still there."

We follow the flow of people heading toward the back on the right side of the house.

The backyard is just as crazy as the front. Party-goers are enjoying the Olympic-size swimming pool with multiple corkscrew slides. Steam billows in the air above a hot tub that's at least fifteen feet long. The hot tub is close enough to the back of the house that half of it is covered by the patio's wood awning.

Concrete takes up most of the backyard, and in the distance, where the edge of the grassy backyard meets sand, is a line of men and women hula dancing by a roaring fire. All the dancers are dressed in grass skirts and the women wear coconut bras.

Even though the sun is setting, the bonfire, tiki torches, and outdoor party lights have the area fully lit. I eye the party guests knowing Tilly was right to have me wear what I am. I would have been the only person in jeans. Half the guests are walking around in swimwear. It's hot enough for it. I pull the black shirt off and tie it around my waist.

"Over here," Tilly says, waving me toward Rocco at the edge of the hot tub.

"Ladies," Rocco says, lazily grinning. "Come on in. Do you need a suit?" He gestures to a clothing rack with hundreds of bathing suits hanging from it by the French doors.

The blonde on Rocco's right doesn't acknowledge us but the brunette on his left glares. Logan's next to her, chatting with a mocha-skinned beauty. I glance at Tilly who is smiling wide, but she can't fool me. Her fingers twirl the tips of her hair, something she does when she feels uncomfortable. And it sucks for me because I'm ready to get out of here.

"Where are the drinks?" I ask Rocco while scanning the backyard because I'm going to need several.

"Tiki hut," Logan says, pointing to the far-right corner of the patio.

It's small and barely lit, but it's there, and so is a line. "You coming?" I ask Tilly. "Or you good here?"

She looks toward the tiki hut and then back to Rocco before focusing on me. "I'm going to grab a suit. Grab me a drink?"

I nod. "Meet you back here in a minute."

"Hey, Tilly," Rocco says, climbing out of the hot tub as she turns her back. "Wait up. I'll walk with you."

Tilly's hand falls away from her hair as Rocco takes her side. Good boy. Don't hurt my sister, or I'll cut you up. While they head toward the house, I make my way through the crowd. I hate this party. If Tilly seems comfortable after I grab drinks, I'm out.

My feet stop when I see Nick walking this way from the fire. He's surrounded by girls and the frown on his face makes me laugh. Looks like Nick doesn't like all the attention. Aiden comes into view along with Casey. They are equally as surrounded, but Casey seems to be enjoying the attention, unlike Aiden.

I watch them head toward the house, and I move to get in line at the tiki hut. There are five bartenders crammed into the little hut, and it looks like all they are serving is slushy type drinks which are a no-go for me. That sugary shit fucks with my stomach and makes me sick.

"Hey, where are the other drinks?" I ask the slender brunette in front of me who smells like coconuts, or maybe the smell is in the air.

She brushes silky hair off her shoulder as she turns to face me. "Like what?"

Her voice is nasally, probably because her nose is so small. She's had to have plastic surgery. She resembles a doll. "Beer, whiskey, mixed drinks. Anything other than that." I gesture to the glass a busty blonde holds as she walks past. The drink is pink with a lemon, lime, and cherry placed on the rim of the glass. "Nothing colorful."

Her tiny nose wrinkles. "Beer? I don't know. Maybe inside." Rolling her eyes, she spins around to face the line.

I glare at the back of her head for a moment and then decide to give up on drinks. I squeeze through the crowd again which seems to be growing by the minute. Tilly's in the water next to Rocco. The blonde that was next to him earlier is sitting next to Tilly and they're chatting like best friends.

I squat down and tap her on the shoulder. "Hey, the line was too long for drinks. I'm out." Mimicking a phone, I hold my thumb and pinky next to my ear. "Call me if you need anything. Wait, where's your phone?"

"It's put up with my stuff in Logan's house," Rocco says.

"Want me to walk you back?" Tilly asks, and I shake my head. "K. I'll call if I need anything." She turns back to the blonde and another girl swims over to join their conversation.

She's quick to make friends everywhere she goes. I'm sure when we get to California, she'll be one of the most popular girls in school like she was at home. I still need to talk to her about school.

"Hayley!" Aiden's moving through the crowd to get to me. "You made it. I've been trying to call you."

"I didn't bring my phone. I doubt I'd have heard it anyway. This place is wild," I say, but my eyes are on his friend. Nick is a few paces behind talking to a tanned beauty. Giggling, she leans over and rests her hand on his arm. Her gold swimsuit is scraps of material and of course the bottom is a thong. Her ass is on the smaller side, but she looks good.

Nick's gaze finds mine. His face remains neutral,

not giving away anything, but his eyes betray him. I know my eyes are saying the same thing. Our attraction to each other goes beyond what I've experienced before. Fucked-up people can always sense their comrades, but with Nick, it's different. There's more. My body knew right away, even if he was being a total jackass.

"I didn't realize it was going to be like this. I should have known. Miller is always over the top." Aiden glances over my shoulder. "Speaking of."

I twist around to see who must be Miller. The guy approaching is lean and tall. He's got perfect six-pack abs and toned legs and arms like most of the guys here. His brown hair is short and styled to stick up in the front. His brown eyes are trained on me, and his lips are pulled into a mischievous smirk. Seeing him now, and hearing the things I did today, makes him easy to read. He's a playful troublemaker.

"I told him you and Tilly are my second cousins."

"Yeah, Nick told me. From Oregon, right?" I glance up at Aiden to see him nod and then move my attention back to Miller. His nose is kind of narrow. It reminds me of a bird's beak.

"Hello, Aiden's cousin." Miller's smooth voice floats through the air. His tongue swipes across his bottom lip. "Are you enjoying the party?"

"The name is Hayley and not really." I turn back to Aiden. "Will you check on Tilly occasionally? I'm headed back."

Miller's hand brushes against my arm. "Leaving? Have you had a drink yet?" Miller steps closer, leaving only a foot or two between us.

"That colorful sugary shit isn't my thing, and I'd need the strong stuff to put up with this."

"Want me to walk you back?" Nick's rough voice sends tingles down my spine.

Still keeping Miller in my peripheral, I turn slightly to face Nick. He's moved closer to me, the girl still in the same spot, her arms crossed, and hazel eyes narrowed.

"Ask and you shall receive," Miller says, snatching a drink from a passing silver tray. "Long Island iced tea?" He hands me the drink and winks.

I wrap my lips around the straw. It's strong, but exactly what I was looking for. I hold the glass up. "Thanks, a drink for the road."

"Or stay, have fun," he says. "Hey, Nick." Miller lifts his chin in greeting.

"Come help me find Casey and then we'll walk back with you." Aiden settles his arm over my shoulders to steer me toward the pool. "Thanks for the invite, Miller. Catch ya later," he throws over his shoulder.

Nick falls in step on my other side, leaving the bronzed beauty all alone as we brush past her.

"Wait." Miller steps up, keeping pace with us. "Why rush? You two should chill. I heard the royals were coming in." Miller's nose wrinkles. "You'll be under a microscope, Aiden. You should let loose." He pats Nick on the back and the muscles in Nick's jaw flex. "You too, Nick."

Nick implied Miller can't be trusted, but it seems like it goes beyond that. Miller must have done something in the past. I finish off my drink and set it onto one of the patio tables as we pass by.

"Where'd you hear that?" Aiden asks Miller, his arm slipping away from my shoulders only to be replaced by Nick's.

That has me tensing up. My gaze slides to Aiden, but he's focused on Miller. I pop my shoulder trying to knock Nick's arm away, but he adds pressure and glares down at me. "What the hell?" I silently mouth, but he doesn't respond.

"Heard Logan and Rocco talking about it. If Hayley's from your dad's side, they probably aren't going to be very happy she's there." His calculating gaze assesses me again. "It's a little freaky how alike you two look." He tilts his head to the side. "Second cousins, you say?"

"There you guys are," Casey says, approaching us with an entourage. "Tilly and Rocco are heading over to the pool. You guys coming?"

"Good idea. Enjoy the pool," Miller says, smiling at me. "Excuse me." With a wink he leaves, heading toward the tiki bar.

"So, you guys want to check out the pool?" Casey asks again.

"Hayley!" My sister waves at me from a group of scantily clad teenagers. "I thought you were leaving?" She grins and skips over to me with a drink in her hand. "Stay with me for a little bit. Have some fun for once." She takes my arm and pulls me close. "Please, please, please. I'll help you pick out a suit. Just thirty minutes. Please." She leans in closer. "The brunette in the black bikini keeps hitting on Rocco. I need backup."

I see the girl she's talking about. It's the girl that was next to him in the hot tub earlier. I grab the Long Island from her. "I'm going to need this if I'm staying longer. Thirty minutes." I gesture toward the group she abandoned. "Go, Rocco is looking lonely. I'll meet you at the pool, and take it easy on the drinks, they're strong," I add, not that she's big on drinking anyway.

"Yay! Thank you, and hurry up. There's a changing room tent thingy you can change in." She smiles wide and then hurries away.

"Guess that means we're swimming," Casey says, nudging me.

"Guess so. I'm gonna change real quick," I tell the guys and then make my way over to the rack of swimwear. I sip the drink I took from Tilly and flick through the suits. There are a few one-pieces but most of what I'm seeing are bikinis.

"Try this." Miller holds up a pink thong bikini.

I finish off my drink. "I'll pass."

"Your eyes are identical to Aiden's. I can tell you two are related."

"Here." I pass him my empty glass since he's still standing there. Toward the end of the rack is a red one-piece in my size. The top makes a sharp

V but it will cover more than the bikinis. I scan the area for the changing room Tilly was talking about. There's a small white tent and several girls are in line for it. I don't have a lot of patience. I look down at the suit and then over at the pool, debating on whether I should bail. I'd much rather spend time under the stars at the beach than here.

"There's a private bathroom. Aiden and Nick used it earlier. It's only for family and close friends." Miller gestures toward the house. "Over here."

"Okay. Thanks." I follow Miller to a back door. He punches a code into a small box. A green light flashes on the handle and Miller pushes the door open. He gestures for me to go ahead and then motions toward the right. The hall is lengthy and quiet. The noise from the party is barely audible.

"This door. Let me make sure they cleaned up after themselves. Hold on." Miller pushes open a white door on the left and comes out a few seconds later. "My brother let his friends change in there. The floor's wet, so be careful."

"I got it. Thanks." I move into a moderately sized bathroom. There are small puddles of water on the white tile, but it's clean and private, so I swap my clothes for the swimsuit. It's a little too tight in certain areas but it works for the most part. I pile my clothes into a ball on the counter and then move back into the hallway. "I could have found my way back. You didn't have to wait."

"I was thinking about your eyes." He looks me

over with a hooded gaze.

I narrow my eyes at his cheesy pickup line. I glance to the right. We're alone and nobody knows I'm here. He better not try to be a creep. I don't feel like fighting in a swimsuit my boobs are already spilling out of. "Well, I'm ready. Wanna lead the way back to the pool?"

"Hold on." He moves into the bathroom only to come back out a second later. "Your eyes are an exact match to Aiden's." He smiles. "Did you know Aiden has his grandmother's eyes?"

"Cool," I say flatly. "Thanks for the trivia." I begin to walk, and unfortunately, he follows.

"His grandmother on his mother's side. How's that be possible when Aiden said you're related on his dad's side?"

I stiffen but keep walking toward the door that's only ten feet away.

"I guess it could be possible if you were his sister."

I don't respond. I don't know what to say. I reach for the door, but Miller's heavy hand lands there first, pushing so I can't pull it open. He slides in between me and the door. Not liking this situation, I swiftly take a few steps back.

"What a scandal it would be if a video of a naked Anna Westling popped up online. Long-lost princess caught stripping at a party." He pulls his phone from his pocket and stares at the screen. "Gorgeous body, by the way."

I scoff. "You recorded me in the bathroom?"

He grins like he's won a prize. "Agree to date me and I'll delete it."

My eyes widen. That is not what I was expecting him to say. "What?"

"I'm trying to jump start my music career, and this will get me the publicity I need. Go out with me a few times, make it look like we're dating. I'll even let you be in one of my videos."

"Or what, you'll post the shit you recorded in the bathroom? Dude, nudity is not taboo anymore. It's everywhere. Put up your little video. People will judge it, and then they'll move on. I don't give a fuck." I glare at him, angry as fuck this asshole is trying to gain something by blackmailing me. "Now let me the fuck out the door."

He narrows his eyes but slides to the side. Still glaring at him, I yank the door open and storm out, but he's not done with me.

"What if I announced your little secret right now?"

I stop mid-stride to glare at Miller who has a stupid smirk on his face. I can only imagine what would happen if he announced it right now. Anna Westling might be the world's most talked-about person. They teach about her and the royal family in public school. Everyone knows the story of the kidnapped princess. The crowd here would go nuts. They'd swarm me.

Miller holds out his hand. "Do we have a deal?"

"Sure," I lie, placing my hand into his. I need to get the hell out of here.

He tightens his grip on my hand and tugs me a step closer. He smells like booze and chlorine. I yank my hand away and move to step away, but he wraps his arm around my waist.

He chuckles. "Calm down, feisty girl. Let's seal our deal with a kiss." He holds up his phone. "I'll post it once your family announces your homecoming. I'm guessing they plan to do it soon?"

I maneuver out of his hold and smile, but I'm not amused. I'm trying not to provoke him. "I'll take a raincheck on that kiss." I move to walk away, but he catches me around the waist again, this time pulling me against him, so my chest is flush with his. I instantly shove him back. "Don't." My eyes are wide and alert.

He taps at the screen on his phone. "A mass text it is."

"No, wait!" I grind my teeth. The idea of kissing this asshole has me pissed off, but all these people crowding in on me would be worse.

"There you are." Nick steps next to me. "Rocco's sick. We're all leaving. Tilly and Casey are walking him back now."

Miller licks his lips and winks at me. "Hayley and I are hanging out."

"He's blackmailing me," I say. Normally I don't bring in other people to fight my battles, but this one is bigger than me. "If I don't kiss him, he's going to tell everyone here I'm Anna." I look away from Miller's wide eyes and slack jaw to see Nick's face turning an ugly shade of red. "Oh, and he has a video of me undressing in the bathroom. He hid his phone while I was changing." I wink at Miller.

"Whoa!" Stepping back, Miller lifts his arms in the air. "I didn't do that shit, Nick. I think she's had too much to drink."

Nick swipes the phone from Miller's hand and pockets it. "Sounds exactly like something you'd do." Nick's arm darts out, his hand wrapping around Miller's throat. Miller's eyes widen as Nick's grip tightens. "We only put up with you because we like Logan," Nick growls.

All the muscles in Nick's arm are flexed, and Miller's face is turning red. I wonder if I should jump in and stop Nick? I take a step forward but pause. I'll give it a little longer. Miller's an asshole.

"This is your last warning, Miller. I will bury you. Do not fuck with us," Nick says, releasing Miller's throat.

With wide eyes, Miller sucks in air and coughs. Nick turns to the side, and I think he's going to walk away, but then his arm swings forward like lightning, and his heavy fist connects with Miller's jaw creating an audible crack. Miller stumbles back several steps, almost falling on his ass. He cusses, holds his face, and narrows his eyes, but doesn't say anything or move to retaliate.

Nick's hand wraps around my upper arm and then we're moving through the crowd. That outcome was so much better than what I had pictured was going to happen. Dammit, Nick can throw a punch. That was fucking hot. His jaw is clenched, his eyes are narrowed slits, and sweat drips down his face, as we speed walk toward the beach.

I shake his arm off as we wind around the crowd surrounding the hula dancers.

When we make it to the beach where it's quiet and the only light comes from the moon and stars, Nick catches my wrist to stop me. "Did he hurt you?" His nostrils flare. "Touch you?"

"I'm fine," I say, my voice sounding breathless and girly. I can't help it. My adrenaline mixed with Nick's badass has me turned on.

He inspects my face and then his gaze travels down my body. I like the way his eyes light up when he takes in the suit. I'm not proud of my body because I don't do much to make it the way it is, but I know I look good. Not as good as the bronzed beauty, but good enough. The suit shows off all my genetic assets. I guess the greasy food I regularly consume might play a role. My thighs are thick but toned and my ass round. My stomach isn't flat as a pancake, but I like it the way it is.

Nick's gaze moves to the V in my suit and then he meets my eyes. I can't help but smile. He's looking at me the way I was looking at him when I first saw him with his shirt off. I bite the inside of my cheek to stop myself from grinning like a damn fool.

I cock my head to the side as the outline of two people appear a few yards away only to slip back into the shadows. I flick my head in the direction of Miller's house. We're too far away to see it, but the light from it radiates into the sky like a beacon. "What about Aiden? Is he with Casey?" I think I see the figures again but only for a second.

Nick clears his throat. "He's at Miller's. We split up to look for you." He pulls out his phone, taps at the screen, and then pockets it. "Just told him to meet us back at the house. Figured we needed to get out of there before I killed Miller."

"Do you and Aiden have beef with Miller?" I ask as we walk beside the water. Someone's house is on our right, but all the lights are off. Each house on this strip has its own little private beach.

"There's history there I don't want to get into." Nick cracks his knuckles. "If he would have announced it there, I would have killed him. He was putting you at risk." He looks me over as we continue a lazy pace. "Once word gets out you've been found, things are going to be different."

"Maybe the world won't like what they see, and they'll get bored of me."

"I don't think anyone can look at you and not like what they see."

My brows raise at his compliment. I turn my head to look at him, but he's focused on the beach ahead. "I don't look like a princess, Nick. They want a princess."

"I think the world has too many princesses," he mumbles.

Footsteps from behind has us turning to see who's coming. Aiden is jogging toward us, popping our intimate little bubble.

"How's Rocco?" Aiden asks, running his hand through his hair.

The gel normally keeping his hair in place is losing its hold. His hair is falling loose around his ears. I think it looks better the way it is now, free.

"Logan said he was pretty trashed," Nick says. "He needs to sleep it off."

"You okay, Hayley?" Aiden asks, eyeing me as we start to walk again.

"Just ready for bed." I see the Westling mansion two houses up, but it feels like it's five miles away.

"I hear that. Me too," Aiden says.

"All right, grandma and grandpa, let's get you two tucked in," Nick says, and Aiden and I shove him forward.

CHAPTER 19

I wake up the next morning after the party and narrow my eyes. I'm comfortable. Like lying on a cloud comfortable. I scoot off the bed, pull back the white sheet, and press my hand to the soft mattress. This has to be new. I climb back onto the bed and roll around. Yeah, this is definitely new or I'm going crazy.

I grab my phone from beside me. Tilly messaged over an hour ago saying she was heading downstairs to eat. She probably won't be there now. I've hardly seen her since we made this our temporary home. Her and Rocco were asleep in her room when I got back last night. I would have flipped my shit, but they were fully clothed, and Rocco had the trash can pushed up next to the bed. I think she had him sleep with her in case he needed someone in the middle of the night.

I pull up the news and then social media, but I don't see what I was expecting. Miller's smarter than he looks or just that scared of Nick. I'm a normal person for a few more days or maybe forever because I refuse to recite a speech on national television. Hopefully I'll become the Westling's dirty little secret.

I pile my hair on top of my head and then throw on comfortable clothes. I kick shoes out of my way so I can open the bedroom door and then cross the hall to Tilly's room. I stop in her doorway, taking in the made bed and clean room. Her phone is on the dresser because she's engrossed in this new life. I haven't heard her talk about any of her friends back home. She seems happy, but when it comes to her, that doesn't always mean she is. She's the type to bottle it all up.

Stepping out into the hall, I shut Tilly's door and then make my way downstairs. As my feet hit the last step, I hear a high-pitched voice. I pause, leaning forward and trying to hear what room the voice is coming from, but it's quiet again. The last thing I want is to run into Nora, so I wait a few more seconds before continuing toward the kitchen.

"I don't have time for this," Nora hisses as she storms out of the kitchen and into the hall where I've stopped.

I hold my breath as she brushes past me, greeting me with a snarl. I shake my head and step into the kitchen. If I'm under the same roof as her for two months, I'll end up snapping on her ass. Aiden's next to the island. His eyes are focused, and brows pinched together as he types something on his phone. I grab a cinnamon roll from a glass dish on the counter, and bite into the soft roll. Gooey icing drips down my chin, so I use my finger to wipe it away.

"How much did you hear?" Aiden asks, setting his phone down.

I swallow the piece in my mouth and lick the icing from my finger. "I didn't hear anything. Just saw Nora tearing through the house as usual. You okay?" I grab a napkin and take another small bite.

"I want to take a semester off, but she acts like it'll be the end of the fucking world if I do."

"Why do you wanna wait?" He gives me a sheepish look, and I arch a brow. "Ah, because of me?"

"You just got here. Leaving for school feels... wrong."

"Your dad said the school was near the house, so you could come home on weekends and stuff, right?"

"Yeah, it's a thirty-minute drive."

"That's not far. You should go." He shouldn't change his life for me. I don't plan on being around long anyway.

"Yeah, maybe. What about you? Are you planning on college?"

"Eventually."

Why is this so awkward for me? He's willing to give up his first semester of college to spend time with me, and I want to leave. I feel a little guilty but it's only because I'm in the same room with him. Once I walk away, the guilt will too. I've built walls of steel around my heart, not letting anyone new in for a long time.

"If you wanted to get in this semester, it wouldn't be a problem."

I fidget with my lip ring. "John mentioned that, but I'm not going to college this semester." The way his expression shifts from hopeful to disappointed has me looking away from him. I should remind him I won't be around long enough to finish a semester. "But anyway, I was grabbing a bite before I went outside to check on Tilly." Keeping my eyes averted from Aiden, I step past him. I've lost my appetite, so I toss my breakfast into the trash on my way to the back door.

"Hey," Aiden says, stopping me as I reach for the doorknob. "If you ever need to talk, I'm here."

Keeping my back to him, I say a quick, "Thanks," and then I'm out the door. The heat from the sun floods my face, and I instantly begin to sweat. The breeze that skates across my skin is hot and sticky. I loathe humidity.

As I head toward the water, I'm focused on the brown-headed boy who has my sister in his arms. I watch as he tosses her into the air. Laughing, she drops into the water and then pops up. She spots me and waves. I wave back, wondering what's wrong with me. Tilly has been having a blast since we got here, and I want to go home.

I watch Tilly, Logan, and Rocco play in the waves for about an hour before heading inside and going up to my room. The beach is pretty, but the gritty sand and salty air leave me feeling like a film has coated my skin and hair.

I give Nana a call but she's on her way to bingo, so I tell her I'll call her later. She doesn't bring up anything about the Westlings. Aunt Kathy said she'd tell her, but maybe she didn't, or maybe Nana doesn't care. I wish I could call Dad. I don't see how no contact with family can be good for him. He must miss us as much as we miss him.

I'm lost in my head while I go through the motions of showering, dressing, and then brushing my hair. I inspect my outfit of choice in the full-length mirror. I went full Nora approved clothes with high-waisted cloth shorts and a flowery curtain material fitted crop top. I don't know why I'm trying, but Nora's crazy-ass better appreciate this. I'm sure tomorrow will be a struggle when I refuse to wear whatever she tries to assign me to meet her family in.

I leave my room with no clear destination in mind and end up in the library. I read the titles of several books I've never heard of. Some of the books look old, but most look like they've never been read. Leave it to rich people to have a library full of books for aesthetics. I hear Nora's heels clicking across the tile in the library before she comes into view.

"There you are." She inspects me with a scrutinizing gaze. "Maybe once we're back in California you can start meeting with a personal trainer. Are those breast implants?"

I frown. "What? No."

"A breast reduction can help with that. You'll fit into clothes better."

"You want me to cut off my boobs so my shirts look better on me?" I stare down at my chest. At best, I'm a small C.

"There's Claire." She snaps her fingers as Claire's passing by with her arms full of long gray zip-up bags. "Over here! How many full-length dresses did you bring?"

"Four, ma'am," Claire says.

"Let me see."

Claire looks ready to collapse, so I offer to help. She hands me two zippered bags. She's only unzipped one of the bags in her arms halfway when Nora says, "Next."

Claire's fingers fumble with the zipper on the second bag. But she manages to pull out a simple floor-length dress. It's light blue and looks silky to the touch. It's similar to the dress I first met Nora in.

"That one. It'll go with Aiden's shirt. Put it in her room and take the other dresses back."

"Yes, ma'am." Claire takes the bags from me and then hurries from the room.

"Take out your piercings when Claire does your makeup in the morning. You need to be up by six."

This bitch. I grind my teeth. "I get you want to impress your family, so I'll wear the dress even though I don't like to wear dresses, but I'm not going to change myself in any other way." I'm putting my foot down on my piercings.

She leans forward, her nostrils flaring. "We both know you're not my daughter."

I chew on my lip ring. She straight-up admitted she doesn't think I'm Anna. What the fuck? Why is she going through all of this then?

"Did you think you'd waltz in and reap my daughter's benefits without accepting her role? Everyone in this family has a duty to uphold. Our name and image are priority. You will get your act together, young lady, or else."

With that, she stomps away. Damn, I think she needs her medication adjusted again. She's lucky she's crazy and not just a rude bitch or I'd smack her. I still might, but I'm going to try extra hard not to.

I make my way to Aiden's room, knocking on the door when I get there. Nick opens it a second later. I brush past him and march up to Aiden who is lounging on the couch with a lit joint in his hand. He looks like the boy the media sees online with the scowl on his face and narrowed eyes. The smoke from the joint slowly swirls in front of his face.

"Nora doesn't think I'm Anna," I say, plucking the joint from his fingers. I take a hit and then pass it back.

Aiden straightens and hands the weed to Nick who drops next to him. "Why do you think that?"

I blow out a cloud of smoke and drop down to the chair. "Um, she straight-up told me."

Aiden swipes the joint back before Nick can hit it. "You must have misunderstood her."

"She was very clear." I lean forward. "Have you noticed the way she says Anna when she's talking to me?"

Aiden gives me a look like he doesn't know what I'm talking about. I know I can't be the only one that hears her condescending tone.

"Listen, I think we should do that second test now, like right now."

Aiden blows out smoke in a long stream. "You're not having doubts, are you? Not after we confirmed parts of your childhood."

"What if the people who took me were like brainwashing me or something? They could have put the memories there or recreated them somehow. They seem like real memories but maybe they aren't?" I turn to Nick because he is the one most likely to understand. "What if I'm not her? You said a mother would know."

Nick doesn't answer but his brows pinch together like maybe he's reconsidering I'm Anna.

"Let's do the second test. It'll help me move forward and maybe help Nora as well," I say to Aiden.

"Yeah, okay," Aiden says, dropping the roach into his nearly empty water bottle. "If it will help you. Let me call James and see if he can arrange something today."

I wait patiently while Aiden speaks with James and Nick scrolls through his phone. Nora's behavior has me on edge. She threatened my family to get me here, yet she doesn't believe I'm her daughter? It doesn't make sense.

"James is on his way up. Since Dad isn't here and I'd rather not bother Mom, I'll swab my cheek to prove relation."

"That works."

Aiden moves to his bed where an open suitcase is next to a pile of crumpled clothes. "Mom's insisting I pack today. She wants to leave for California as soon as her family leaves." He shoves clothes into the suitcase. "Nick's mom is fine with taking time off. I thought that would help my case with Mom."

Nick pockets his phone. "I'm only taking off one semester. It helps I've finished a year already." Nick grins. "And someone needs to be there to keep Casey on track."

"Why not do what you want?" I say. "You're an adult, Aiden. She can't tell you what to do."

He's quiet for a moment, and then says, "At least Nick will be around so you won't be completely alone." Aiden shoves more clothes than what can fit into his bag.

"Oh, you live nearby?" I ask Nick.

"He's staying at our house in California." Aiden smashes the top of the suitcase closed and leans onto it to zip it up.

Nick licks his lips. "Aiden asked me to."

"Really? Why?"

"You shouldn't be alone all the time," Aiden mumbles, launching the bag toward the door, it hits with a loud thud.

"I don't mind being alone. Sometimes it's better that way."

Aiden and Nick glance at each other. There's a knock at the door, and then James is walking in, handing Aiden and I each a swab. He doesn't ask questions, just takes the swabs from us once we've swabbed our mouths and then leaves the room.

"Is he like your maid?" I ask Aiden who's mumbling obscenities as he packs another bag.

"He's more my security but was my head guy in finding you."

"He knew about the mark and Nick knows," I say. "Anyone else? Does Casey? If you've told people, it's possible others know, or your parents have told others. Maybe someone was grooming me to one day claim to be Anna."

"Why would they do that?" Aiden asks, chucking the lumpy bag at the door from across the room.

"Money. People will do anything for money," I say, eyeing him cautiously as he begins angrily cramming shoes into a small suitcase.

Nick frowns. "The weed was supposed to calm him down."

Aiden slings the shoe bag toward the door and then storms into the closet.

"I'm gonna grab Tilly. I need to talk to her about school choices." My gaze trails Aiden as he shoots out of the closet fighting with an armful of clothes still attached to the hangers. "Let me know when you get the results back." I grasp the doorknob. "And Aiden might need some more weed."

CHAPTER 20

I head downstairs, moving toward the kitchen to grab a snack before asking Tilly to come in from the water. She's going to be so fucking excited about attending school in California. Even if it's only for a couple of months and then she has to switch back to her old school. I stop abruptly when I step through the kitchen entrance. Nora is sitting with my sister at the island, and they're alone. My guard is instantly up.

Tilly sees me and lights up. "Guess what? You're never going to believe it."

"What?" I ask, straining to keep my eyes on my sister when I want to glare at Nora.

"I'm going to an art school in England! Nora set it up for me. I'll be studying under renowned artists. Can you believe it?"

Don't explode, I tell myself. Stay calm. This is a good opportunity for my sister. "Why the fuck didn't you talk to me about this first?" I glare at Nora, my heart pounding against my chest.

214

Nora's eyes widen and she slowly stands. "Excuse me?"

Tilly jumps up. "Hayley, it's fine. Don't do this, please."

She's sending my sister away to get back at me. "You want to send my sister to a boarding school across the world?" My voice shakes with emotion. I'm going to kill her. I'm going to grab a fucking knife and slit her goddamn throat. My pounding heart fills my ears.

"It's an amazing opportunity, Hayley. It's only for my sophomore year, and I'll be able to visit on holidays and breaks."

"Wow," I say to Nora. "You planned this fast. Why not send me away too? Why am I here?"

Nora smiles. "I have other plans for you, *daughter*."

"Excuse me? If you think I'm going to stay here and take this shit, you are fucking crazy." I step up to get in Nora's face, but Tilly grips my shoulders and pushes me back. My hands fist at my side. Heat floods my body. I'm about to explode. I'll deal with the fall out of my dad being questioned by police and possibly imprisoned, but I won't take Nora shipping my sister to another country.

"God, Hayley! Shut up! Nora's been so nice, and you're mad at the world and taking it out on everyone around you!" A sob breaks free. "You're ruining everything. Why can't you be happy for once?" Crying, she runs out of the kitchen.

"You're messing with the relationship I have

with my sister. That wasn't part of the agreement," I growl.

"I offered her an amazing opportunity. I don't see how that's harmful to your relationship with her."

Rocco pauses inside the doorway. "Hey, what's the matter with Tilly? She looked like she was crying."

"I'm tired. I need to lie down," Nora says, losing the bite to her tone she had before Rocco walked in. "Try the dress on, *Anna*. I'll see you later."

"I'm not trying the dress on. I'm fucking leaving."

Nora's hand jolts out to snatch my wrist as I brush past her. "You listen here," she says through a clenched jaw. "I thought I made myself clear. Do as you're told, and we'll get along just fine. I would hate for the police to visit your father at Franklin Creek Rehabilitation and Recovery."

She releases me and storms away. The fact she knows where my dad is, has my stomach dropping to my feet.

"What was that about?" Rocco asks.

"That bitch is crazy," I say. "Seriously, she needs to be locked away. What the fuck?"

Rocco calls after me as I dart away. I race up the stairs, sprint down the hall, and rush into Tilly's room. I'm out of breath when I reach her and can't say what I need to right away.

"Hold on," I wheeze. I fan my face and she glares at me from her bed. "I know you'd love to go to art school." Groaning, I hold my side. I'm really out of shape. "Accepting the benefits that come with living here are not worth it. Nora threatened Dad unless I agreed to stay here for two months."

"No, she didn't," Tilly says, clutching a pillow to her chest. "You said we were coming to visit, and we'd be back in time for me to start school."

"I said that because I didn't want to worry you."

"Just like what you said about them asking you to get naked at the interview?" She shakes her head. "You don't think I'm ready to go by myself. You know how much I love art and design." She smooshes a pillow to her face and cries into it. "You're ruining my life."

Tilly can be the happiest person ever, but she can also be extremely dramatic. "Tills, I love you, and I wish it was about the school but it's not."

She lifts her head from the pillow. "You're being selfish. You don't want to be alone, and nobody will put up with your bitchy attitude but me." Tears pour down her reddened cheeks.

"You don't mean that, Tilly. You're mad." I hope she doesn't mean that. I'm not that bad. I know I've been a little different since Mom died, but I'm fucking trying. "I'm not going to stay here and put up with whatever Nora has planned, we need to go, now."

"What?"

Aiden's the one to question what I said. Tilly focuses on him as he steps into her room with Nick and Casey following behind.

"We heard yelling," Casey says.

"You're leaving? James hasn't called with the results yet. The lab is local. It won't take long. Can't you wait a little longer?" Aiden asks, clutching the phone in his hand.

"It's not about that. Nora wants to send my sister away."

"To a top-rated art school in England," Tilly snaps, wiping away tears. "Things are finally going good for me and you want to ruin it," she throws at me. "You will never be happy. You'll always be miserable and want to drag me down with you!"

"You're pissed off I haven't been happy? When did I have time to be? Mom died and Dad checked out. I had to step up so your life wouldn't change. There was grocery shopping, meal planning, laundry, cleaning, lists, emails, bills. I was fucking exhausted all the time and stressed to the max." I'm hot everywhere and my hands are shaking.

And the woman who loved me unconditionally, who I loved with all my heart, was suddenly gone. It shattered me. I don't say that part out loud because it leaves me too vulnerable.

"I didn't ask you to do that!"

The guys look uncomfortable as hell, and I feel like I'm going to snap. "Fine, Tilly. Do whatever the fuck you want to do, but I'm leaving. I'm going back to Nana's house."

"Are you serious?" Aiden asks in disbelief.

My stomach clenches with guilt. "I can't do this, Aiden. We can keep in touch. I'll visit whenever you want me to, and you can come to mine. I just can't stay here."

"Tilly said you guys aren't even close to your grandmother," Aiden says. "I thought you'd wait and leave when your dad went home. Mom talked to his doctor and they said it could be a while."

"She talked to his doctor?" My chest rises and falls rapidly.

Aiden frowns. "I guess so. I know she can be complicated. She needs time—"

"She's beyond complicated! She's nuts."

"She has issues she's working on. We all want you here. What about Dad, Colt, and Liv? We need you," Aiden practically pleads.

"What about what I need? I need my sister to be here with me. I miss my job and my friends."

"It'll take time—"

"No, this is being forced on me. The only reason I'm here is because she threatened to send investigators after my family. My dad—"

"That's the only reason you're here?" Aiden snaps, his nostrils flaring. "I told you I'd talk to her about it, but you said not to. You didn't care about getting to know us?" He angrily shakes his head. "Fine—"

"Aiden—"

"No, you should go. Tilly should still get to go to England though." He turns to her. "I'll fund the school for you even if my mom changes her mind." He glances at his phone as it lights up. "Test came back, same as before, not that you care."

He barrels out the door, and Tilly screams at me to get out of her room.

"Aiden!" Casey hollers, but Aiden doesn't look back.

Nick looks like he wants to say something, but he doesn't as I push past him to go to my room. I grab my clothes from the back of the closet, shoving them into my duffle bag but the hangers are still on, so it's a big fucking mess. I sink to the floor, sitting cross-legged and drop my face into the palms of my hands as a stupid tear breaks free.

CHAPTER 21

It doesn't take long until my face is covered in salty wetness, and I'm a blubbering mess. I hate fighting with Tilly. I hate that she thinks that shit about me. I hate I'm here and not at home.

Feeling someone's presence as they slip into my room, I glance up and see Nick standing above me. I can barely see him through my teary eyes. My mom always encouraged crying, but I fucking hate it. It makes me feel like a weak bitch.

"Everything's screwed up. Nora doesn't believe I'm Anna, and she's trying to change me into something I'm not. I wish my mom was here. I wish she'd never gotten into her car or the idiot who smashed into her hadn't been drinking." Tears roll down my face. I know if my mom was here, things would be better. I hate the jerk who ended her life. He got a slap on the wrist because he knew people in high places. I should have taken my revenge to the next level but I was lucky I didn't get caught doing what I did.

Nick drops down next to me. He pulls me against his side and then gently brings my head down to his shoulder. His arm moves behind my back to land on my hip. The comfort he's providing feels better than crying alone, so I lean into him and bring my knees to my chest. He's patient while every single tear is released.

"I'm really her. I wasn't sure, but I'm Anna. I thought the second test might say otherwise." I wipe my nose. "This is so weird. I never would have thought it." My stomach flutters anxiously. Aiden, Colt, and Liv are my siblings. I kind of like the idea of that. My family is so small. I have a twin fucking brother. I have a twin brother who is pissed off at me.

"It was hard to believe because you didn't want to be her," Nick says.

I nod my head against his shoulder and then groan. "I'm eighteen again. I was so close to being twenty-one."

"Yep, you're practically a baby," he teases. "I think we all pictured the reunion going differently, but we didn't take into consideration that you would have a family and a whole life you liked. We didn't expect you to be thriving."

I wipe the tears from my face. "I wouldn't say thriving, but yeah, I liked my life for the most part."

"What's something you would have changed about it?"

I think for a moment. "Besides my mom's death, college. I took the first semester off, and I've been trying to go since. Something always came up."

"I heard John offered to get you in. You don't want to start with Aiden?"

"My dad," I say, still tucked against Nick's side. "He's in Tennessee. When he gets out of rehab, he'll want Tilly and I home with him."

"Is your dad rooted in Tennessee? Do you think he'd move?"

"Like to California? I don't know." I pull at my lip ring. That hadn't crossed my mind. If my dad was in California, maybe I could give getting to know the Westlings a shot. Everyone besides Nora seems in it for the long haul. My shoulders feel lighter with the thought of giving in.

"Why don't you take it day by day. Don't plan too far ahead. You could take online classes next semester, so you can live anywhere." He pulls a bag of weed and papers from his back pocket. "And I have just the thing to help you relax."

Lifting my head from his shoulder, I laugh. "It's only noon. I'm not ready to be rendered unconscious."

He chuckles. "This isn't the same shit." He pulls out papers and rolls a nice sized joint. "Ladies first." He hands it to me.

The door flies open and Casey barrels in. "Hey!" He plucks the joint from my fingers. "Remember, it's my turn to have quality time with Hayley."

Nick laughs. "Last night was your night. You forfeited."

"No. Last night was the party." He puts the joint to his lips only to frown and hand it back to me. "You can go first. You look pretty rough there, princess."

Nick hands me a lighter, and Casey drops down on my other side. I light up, taking a few hits and then pass it to Casey.

"Damn, your room is messy," Casey says, passing the weed to Nick. "Total opposite of Aiden."

I scan my room. Clothes and shoes are scattered around the floor. My purse is on a chair in the corner and the dresser is covered with hair products, makeup, and maybe a little trash. "Whatever. I like it like this." I take the weed from Nick and hit it a couple times. My worries are already melting away.

Casey blows out a cloud of smoke. "Don't worry, Hayley. Things will work out. It was fate that brought you back, and fate has a way of making things fall into place."

I take the joint from him. "I don't believe in fate."

Casey scoffs. "You shouldn't say that. You're going to piss it off."

I laugh. "Yeah, right." I cup my hands over my mouth. "Do you hear me, fate? I don't believe in you, but on the slim chance you're real, I challenge you."

"Oh shit," Casey whispers. "Like to a duel? You're challenging fate to fight?"

"I'm challenging it to whatever. It's not real, so it doesn't matter."

"Do you think aliens are real?"

I lean my head against the mattress behind me. "Yeah."

"Me too," Casey says, sinking to the floor where he sprawls out on his back. "I watched this alien show before. They talked about government cover-ups and shit. It seemed legit."

Nick moves to the bathroom, and I lower myself to the floor next to Casey. "I saw some weird lights in the sky before. It wasn't a plane. Either it was some secret government drone, or it was aliens."

"Hell ya." Casey laughs. "For real, though. I'd piss my pants if I ever saw an alien."

"Why do you always talk about aliens when you get high?" Nick asks, sprawling out on the floor.

He's inches away from me and staring up at the painting. He's so perfect that he could be a painting come to life.

"It was that or kiss her." Casey laughs. "I see the way you look at her, so I figured aliens were safer." Casey rolls his head to the side to meet my eyes. "He's got it bad for you."

"Shut the fuck up, Casey. This is why nobody likes smoking with you," Nick says, reaching his arm over me to jab Casey in the ribs.

"You weren't supposed to be here, ass. You're butting in on my bonding time with Hayley."

"Can you two shut up. You're ruining my buzz."

I point at the painting above us. "Focus on the ceiling. Who do you think painted that?" The longer I stare at it, the more details I see. One angel has a scroll behind his back and a little smirk on his face. That angel is up to something.

Casey's phone chimes, and he sits up. "Hell ya. Gabby from the party wants to meet up."

"Don't you have a girlfriend?" I ask.

He types something out on his phone. "We aren't exclusive. Too busy for that shit. She's on a world tour right now. I'll see her in a few months." Staring at his phone, he grins. "Looks like we'll have to bond later, princess." He gets to his feet and lightly kicks Nick's foot. "Don't have too much fun without me." Laughing, he shuffles out the door.

My lips feel tingly and then numb.

"You know what's a weird word? Numb," I say, making sure to pronounce the b. "I know the b is supposed to be silent but that's dumb." I laugh. "Numb and dumb."

"Everywhen." Nick says.

"What?"

"Everywhen is a weird word. It means always. Nobody ever uses it."

I lift my head from the floor. He's staring up at the ceiling, his brown hair messier than usual. "I don't know. I kinda like that one."

"If you say it fast, it sounds like everyone." Nick grins and moves to a sitting position with his elbows propped on his bent knees. "Everywhen,

everywhen, everywhen. See, it sounds like everyone."

"Wait, you weren't saying everyone?" I ask, sitting up and gazing into his bloodshot and glossy eyes.

Nick chuckles. "No, I was saying everywhen."

"Everywhen. Oh, yeah. I like that one. How would you use it in a sentence?"

Nick wets his bottom lip as he thinks. "If someone was to ask me how often I think about sex, I'd say everywhen."

We both bust up laughing. His laugh is deep and sexy.

"That's my new favorite word. It's better than numb." I rub my ears. "That was some good weed. My ears are burning. My ears everywhen burn when I smoke good weed. Did I use it right?"

He chuckles. "Yeah. I think so."

"Thanks for the smoke. I feel better."

He strokes my hair. "I got your back, Hayley Anna. Everywhen."

The way his lips move when he says everywhen, makes me want to run my tongue over them and then take his bottom lip into my mouth and suck, maybe even bite. Biting down on his plump bottom lip while having an orgasm would be fucking awesome.

Fuck it. I'm going to kiss him. If he rejects me, which I don't think he will, I can blame it on the high. Weed makes me horny. His lips are moving, but I'm not listening to his words. I scoot closer and then get to my knees so I can touch his lips with mine. They are soft and thick and feel amazing against mine, almost like a lip massage. His hands move to grip my waist, fingers digging into my skin. I knew he wanted this too.

His tongue sweeps into my mouth, and I reciprocate. Our mouths move lazily against each other while our tongues mingle sensually. He pulls me closer, deepening the kiss, and I move to straddle his lap. His hands roam my body, starting at my shoulders and moving down to my waist and then resting on my thighs.

We slowly move from the floor to the bed without breaking the kiss. On our sides, our legs are tangled together and our hands exploring, mine under his shirt to feel his hard abs and pecks.

Kissing, we lay like that for a while before he nudges me onto my back and then slips between my legs. His hard length presses against me in exactly the right spot. I haven't had a make-out session in a long time, and the chemistry between us is like nothing I've experienced before.

A sound at the door has us quickly breaking apart in time to see it pushed open and Casey strutting in with a tub of ice cream and a few spoons. Nick and I glance at each other both wearing the same confused expression.

"Gabby got caught up. She's not ready yet." Casey walks around the bed to drop down next to me seemingly unaware he interrupted us. "I brought ice cream."

I'm a little aggravated because kissing Nick is the best kind of high, but my buzz is wearing off and munchy mode is kicking in. Casey hands us each a spoon and sets the tub of mint chip ice cream in my lap.

"You guys want to roll another?" Casey asks, dipping his spoon into the ice cream tub.

"Nah, I'm good," Nick says.

I shake my head. "I'm okay." I scoop out some ice cream and lick it off the spoon. I notice Nick watching me, so I do it again but more slowly. Nick arches his brow, and I laugh.

"What?" Casey asks, digging out some more ice cream.

"Nothing. So, you into this Gabby chick?" I ask him.

"She's cool."

I pause with my spoon full of ice cream at my mouth. "That's it? She's cool? You seemed excited when you ran out of here earlier."

Nick laughs and spoons out some ice cream.

"I was high. I like getting my dick sucked when I'm stoned. Now I have to wait." He grins and scoops out some more ice cream. "And no worries. She knows it's only a casual hookup." He eats the ice cream off his spoon. "You guys sure you don't want to smoke anymore? My buzz is gone."

Before Nick or I can answer, Casey's phone chimes. He pulls it from his pocket and grins down at the screen.

I smirk. "The casual hookup?"

Casey nods. "Yep. She's pulling up." Casey plucks our spoons from our hands, grabs the ice cream, and darts out the door.

"He could have left the ice cream." The laugh that slips out of me is carefree and happy. It feels good.

Nick smirks. "I agree about the ice cream." He presses his hand firmly down on the mattress. "Much better than the old one."

"Wait, that was you? You changed the mattress?" I laugh. "I thought I was going crazy."

"I had it changed when we were at the party. Your old one was shit."

I smile. "Thanks."

We stare at each other for a moment and then we're moving at the same time. Our lips connect. Nick's hand moves into my hair, grabbing and tugging. The little prickles against my scalp have a breathy moan leaving my lips.

This kiss isn't slow and careful like before. There's more fire to this. His hand slips underneath my shirt, and skilled fingers find the hardened peak of my left breast.

"Fuck, you have some nice tits." He tugs the shirt up. "This needs to come off."

He helps me pull it over my head and toss it to the side. I watch Nick's face as he takes in my bare chest. He smiles and brings his head down to lick and suck my sensitive nipples. I throw my head back and arch into him as he drives me wild.

"How high are you?" he murmurs against my

neck.

"I'm not," I pant, running my fingers through his soft hair.

Pulling back, he grins. "I was hoping you'd say that."

I laugh lightly. "Didn't want to take advantage of me? I never get so stoned or intoxicated that I can't make an informed decision, and FYI, I like to fuck while high."

He nips my bottom lip. "Good to know, princess." His hands come to the hem of my shorts to yank them down. He moves to the side so he can rip them off and then he takes his place between my thighs. He trails kisses over my neck and chest.

"I bet a week ago neither of us would have guessed we'd be in this situation." I smirk.

He chuckles. "Nope."

"Why did you think I wasn't her?"

He meets my eyes. "I had a preconceived idea of what Anna would be like. I thought she would be... timid, and you were intense, fearless, reckless, and so damn beautiful in the glow of the fire. I was trying to intimidate you." He slowly runs his finger over each nipple. "I didn't want to get my hopes up if you weren't Anna, but I hated that you might be her and were at that party with all of those drunk idiots."

"I can take care of myself," I say, slipping my hand into his sweatpants. I wrap my hand around his impressive length and give him a few strokes. I discreetly take my lip ring out while he's focused on my nipples. "I can take care of you too." I flip him over, kneeling next to him as I pull him free. Damn, that's big, and now I'm feeling intimidated about what I'm about to do. I've only ever given my psycho-ex head, and his dick was a lot smaller than this.

Flipping my hair to the side, I lock eyes with Nick as I lower myself to rub my tongue over the tip. With lust-filled eyes, he groans and brings his hand to the back of my head to guide me down farther. We stare at each other as I take my time on him. His thighs clench, and he squeezes his eyes shut. Pleasuring Nick Cabot is fucking hot as hell.

I push myself to take as much of him as I can. He must like that because his hips thrust up to push himself to the back of my throat. My mouth waters which is a good thing in this situation. With one hand on the back of my head, his other hand moves between my thighs to caress me over my black lacy underwear. He slips a finger underneath the fabric and slides back and forth. He rubs my clit for a minute before slipping into me. I moan loudly over his dick while he thrusts into my throat and my center.

I fist his base where my mouth won't go. He's too big to take in all the way. I suck harder while moving my head faster. I don't think I've ever enjoyed giving head as much as I'm enjoying this.

With a growl, he pulls away. "I need to feel you." He flips me onto my back, settles between my thighs, and then pulls my underwear to the side while his fingers play. He kisses me hard and then nips at my bottom lip. I pull his into my mouth and gently suck. I pull away and grin at the sight of his swollen and puffy lips.

"I need inside, Haley," Nick rumbles, but he doesn't move.

"I want this." I wrap my hand around his cock, guiding him toward me as he holds my underwear to the side.

He inches in, the muscles in his back and legs straining. I'm dripping wet, but there's still resistance because he's so damn big. He groans as he pushes forward slowly.

Once he's fully in, he kisses me softly while his hips begin to move. I run my hands over his shoulders, and he pulls his mouth from mine to lick and suck on my nipples. I bend my knees and plant my feet on the mattress so I can rock my hips in time with his thrusts. Each stroke feels amazing and entices breathy moans from me.

I slip my hand between us to circle my clit. Nick begins to thrust a little faster, telling me how good I feel around his dick as he picks up speed. When I'm not able to keep up, I wrap my legs around his waist and tilt my pelvis up.

The sound of our fucking fills my ears. He grabs a handful of my hair and pulls so that my neck is stretched to the side. He nips at my neck, my ear, and then my bottom lip. Goddamn, this feels good. So fucking good. I press against my clit as he thrusts harder and harder, and then I squeeze my eyes shut and cry out as an orgasm rips through me. He slows down his pace as I contract around him.

When I come down from it, Nick pins my wrists above my head and kisses me fiercely as he thrusts in and out.

"Fuck," he grunts against my mouth and then he's pulling out to spill himself on my belly.

I watch his hand as he pumps all of himself out. Sweat drips from his hair to his chest. His tan skin is glistening like the first time I saw him with his shirt off. He's so fucking hot.

Breathing heavily, he drops down next to me, propping himself up on his elbow while I use my shirt to clean myself up. His fingertip starts at my neck and lightly trails between my breasts and then he traces around each sensitive nipple.

"Fucking gorgeous." He leans over and licks each pebbled peak. "And mouthwateringly delicious." His hand moves to cup me between my legs. "I didn't get to taste this, though. Ready for round two?"

I smirk. "I'm always ready."

CHAPTER 22

Nick Cabot has some serious stamina. After round three, he leaves me a boneless mess to head downstairs and grab us water. I quickly rinse off in the shower, my mind replaying how amazing his tongue felt. The memory tempts me to reach down and touch myself, but I'm still so sensitive from the multiple orgasms Nick's mouth graciously gave.

I'm changing into sweats and a tank when there's a knock at the door. "It's unlocked!" I shout as I search the bed for my lip ring. I glance over my shoulder as the door swings open.

Aiden rubs the back of his neck. "Can we talk?"

Seeing him standing in the doorway looking uncomfortable has me remembering the whole reason Nick ended up in my room. What happened with Tilly and Aiden completely slipped my mind. I almost laugh out loud. Nick fucked me into oblivion. I step out into the hall with Aiden, closing the door behind me. My room smells like sex and sweat. "Sure, we can talk. Your room?"

As we approach Aiden's door, Nick steps around the corner holding two bottles of water. "Hey." He holds out a bottle to me and winks. "Thought you might be thirsty."

I lick my lips. "I am. Thank you." I take the bottle from him. Warmth spreads throughout my body as we stare at each other.

"Gonna talk to Hayley for a minute. Think Rocco was looking for you," Aiden tells him. "Him and Tilly were going out somewhere."

"Do you know where?" I ask, peeling my gaze away from the guy with the magic mouth.

Aiden shakes his head. "They didn't say."

"I'll find out and let you know," Nick says.

"Thanks." I wink at him before following Aiden into his room. I should probably feel weird I slept with Aiden's best friend, but I don't. Just like I don't feel bad for sleeping with him after only knowing him for a week. My parents had sex the first day they met and were together every day after that. Not that I think Nick and I will be together forever.

"I wanted to apologize, Hayley." Aiden drops down on the couch.

"Apologize?" I take the chair, glad twins can't read each other's thoughts. I don't think he'd appreciate the graphic details of Nick's mouth between my thighs.

"I wasn't thinking about you at all. Nothing in my life has changed, but for you, everything has."

"Yeah. Everything has."

"I feel like a dick for earlier."

"It's fine. I'll always be honest with you, Aiden. Even if it might hurt your feelings. I'm not leaving yet. I'll stay for the two months as per the agreement with Nora. I want to get to know you, Liv, Colt, and John, but I can't live with you guys forever."

"I get that. Maybe I can check out some colleges in Tennessee next year."

"Really?" I smile, liking the idea of having more family close by, and Aiden is my twin. I have a twin fucking brother. "That would be cool."

"Yeah?" he asks, sounding hopeful. "That doesn't freak you out?"

"No. You're my brother." I lean forward. "Colt too. I want to get to know both of you, but someone should always be around when I'm near Liv. She's a handful."

He laughs. "She is. Sophia is incredibly good with her."

I chuckle and then sigh. "I need to find Tilly. We haven't fought in forever." I get to my feet and so does Aiden.

"One more thing. Tomorrow. Mom's family is intense but they're good people." He rubs his chin. "Rocco said you might bail. I think Tilly mentioned it to him or something."

"Surprisingly, that hadn't crossed my mind. But yeah, I can't guarantee I won't lock myself in my room if they hate me."

"They won't hate you. They'll have opinions about... everything, but they love you."

"They can't love me. They don't even know me."

"Are you worried?"

I scoff and then grin. "No. I don't care if someone doesn't like me. That's life."

He smiles. "They might try to get you to come back with them."

"That's not happening." I back up toward the door. "Let me go find out where my sister is before she does something reckless."

"Okay, so, we're good?"

I nod. "We're good."

I move across the hall to knock on Nick's door, but no answer. My phone's in my room, so I head that way. I push my door open and walk into a nice surprise. Nick is in my bed and shirtless.

"How'd it go?"

I drop down beside him. "Fine. Did you find out where Tilly is?"

"Her and Rocco went for a ride. She needed some space."

"And Rocco to the rescue. I know you said he's a good guy, but he's a sixteen-year-old boy with a life of privilege. My sister is in way over her head." I laugh because I'm in over my head. I've never been the casual sex type, but I don't expect us to commit because we gave in to our urges.

"Stop overthinking everything." Nick grabs me around the waist, pulling me to straddle his lap. "I think you need some stress relief." He kisses and sucks at my neck.

"Hm," I hum, tilting my head to the side to give him better access. "I think I do." Just because I've never done the casual thing doesn't mean there's anything wrong with it. I let Nick relieve me of my stress, and damn if he isn't amazing at it.

CHAPTER 23

I wake up to my alarm going off way too fucking early, but luckily, I actually slept last night. I'm not going to tell Nick. He was cocky enough when he slipped from the room late at night after giving me so many orgasms I lost count.

We didn't use protection. I know I don't have any STDs and Nick said he didn't either. I guess we're already trusting each other. I'm also trusting him to pull out which probably isn't very smart even though Nick insisted it's fine. I might need to look into birth control if we keep this up, even though I hate the side effects it causes me—weight gain, constant headaches, and spotting.

I'm scrubbing my teeth clean when I hear a woman calling my name. I step out of the bathroom and see Claire setting a bulky metal case down on my dresser along with two cups of Starbucks.

"Hi, Hayley. Are you ready to get started?" She

hands me a cup. "Mrs. Westling isn't a fan of coffee, but I thought maybe you were?"

"Yes, a big fan." I take the cup from her and sit on the edge of the bed. "Thank you."

"No problem. I don't see how people function without it."

I take a few gulps of delicious coffee. "By get started do you mean makeup?" She nods. "I like my makeup light, almost non-existent."

"Gotcha. What's your makeup routine like now?"

"Eyeliner and mascara."

"Okay. I'll keep things simple." She winks. "Unlike last time."

I watch as she opens the metal caboodle type case, displaying a makeup store. She examines my skin and then pulls bottles, brushes, tubes, and eye shadow pallets from the case.

She looks up at the ceiling and frowns. "Do you mind doing this in the bathroom? The lighting will be better there. I'm assuming there's a vanity like in the other bathrooms?"

"There is." I head in, kicking my dirty clothes and towels to a corner and then sit down on a cushioned stool while Claire sets everything onto the vanity.

Soft brushes gliding over my skin, Claire's soft humming, and the fact it's not even seven, has me in and out of sleep while Claire works.

"There. Tell me what you think."

I turn around to face the mirror and smile.

"Wow. It's perfect." My skin looks flawless but not fake, my eyes are sparkly and awake. I wouldn't normally wear pink eye shadow, but this is more a gray-pink, and it's applied just right. I place my nose and lip ring back into place.

Claire smiles. "A little rebellious, I see?"

I pop my shoulder. "I'm just being myself. I like my piercings."

Claire pulls the dress from my closet and holds it out to me. "You are going to look stunning. I think your hair would look beautiful pulled up to show off your neck."

"That works. I usually wear it up."

She hangs the dress on the back of the door to take my hair, pulling it in different directions. "I think I have an idea." She smiles. "I'm so lucky I get to work with you. You're the perfect model. So pretty."

I sip my coffee while she styles my hair into something that reminds me of a Viking. There are braids and twists. Parts of my hair are down while others are up. My naturally wild hair seems to work perfectly with this hairstyle.

"What do you think?"

Grinning, I turn my head from side to side while facing the mirror. "I love it. I look like a warrior."

"Exactly, a warrior princess." She gives me a look like she knows exactly who I am, and then she heads into the bedroom while I slip on the dress.

The dress fits snug against my skin and brushes

against my feet. I've never seen a dress like this. There is lace, glitter, and beads. The back is open, so I go bra free.

"Holy shit," Claire whispers. "Sorry, you look... wow."

I move into the room to see myself in the full-length mirror, and Claire is right, wow. I look fucking amazing—fierce. I smile. Nora's going to hate it.

I slowly turn to Claire, careful not to move too fast. "I feel like if I move, my hair will come undone."

"It's not going anywhere. I bobby pinned and hair sprayed the crap out of it. Move freely." I notice something sparkly in her hand and frown.

Claire holds up a crown covered in diamonds. "This is the last piece."

"Yeah, I'm not wearing that."

"It totally goes with the warrior princess look, and Nora will kill me if you don't have it on. Please. I don't want to lose my job," she begs.

I sigh. "Fine. I'll wear it in front of Nora before I take it off."

Claire smiles. "Thank you." She motions for me to sit down. "It'll only take a second."

I drop down to the bed while she places the heavy crown on my head and tightens the strap around the bottom. She steps back, and I swear she has tears in her eyes as she takes me in.

I inhale a deep breath. "I guess I should go check on my sister." I haven't heard from her since our fight. Aiden text me when she got home last night, but I didn't want to push her to talk if she wasn't ready.

Claire nods. "Nicole was assigned to your sister. She's probably ready."

There's a soft knock at the door. "Hayley? Are you in here?"

I instantly tear up. My baby sister looks so grown up. Her dress is light purple and floor-length. Tiny crystal beads cover the heart-shaped top. Her normally straight hair hangs around her shoulders in soft waves, and her bangs have been pinned back with a sparkly clip. "You're beautiful, Tilly. Seriously."

She grins. "You are always beautiful but..." Her eyes cut to Claire.

Claire smiles. "My work here is done. I'll step out and give you two some privacy." She grabs her coffee from the dresser. "I'll come back for my things in a bit."

"You look like a real princess!" Tilly squeals, once we're alone. "I love the crown."

Any concern I had about her being angry with me is gone. "Me? Tilly, you look like a princess and so grown up."

"I am growing up. I'm not a kid anymore, and I want to go to that school, Hayley. It's an amazing opportunity." Her blue eyes sparkle with hope.

I need to let her make her own choices even if they aren't my choices. It's what Mom would have done. "I'll miss you, but you're right, you need to make this choice for yourself." Nora wants her gone, and maybe it's better she isn't around the crazy bitch.

"I was hoping you'd say that. I told Nora to book the ticket. I'm leaving tomorrow."

I feel like the air has been knocked from my lungs. I force a smile even though tears pool in my eyes. "I didn't know it would be so soon. You'll be in another country." My brows draw together. "Doesn't a parent need to sign paperwork for you to go to a different school? How does that work?"

Tilly shrugs. "Nora said she took care of everything."

"Maybe I should go with you for a few days?"

"Rocco's coming with me. His parents have a house near the school. He knows the area and is going to help me get settled."

My eyes widen. "Things are serious between you two? Are you being careful?" One day she's doing makeovers with her friends, and the next, she's falling for a guy.

"Rocco's great. I like spending time with him, but we aren't *there* yet."

I internally sigh with relief. "If you get to that point and have questions, I'm here."

"I think it will be a while. I'm definitely not ready for that. We haven't even kissed."

I find that strange because he's a sixteen-year-old boy who touches my sister every chance he gets. Maybe he's one of those touchy-feely people. Maybe he's not interested in my sister like I thought he was. He'd be an idiot not to be into her.

"Hayley. Are you listening to me?"

I blink. "Yes. No, what?"

"Are you ready? Nora wants us downstairs for breakfast by eight. Your family will be here soon."

"Has Nora been nice to you?"

"I haven't talked to her much besides her offering to pay for school."

"Okay. That's good. If today sucks, let's play food poisoning and meet in my room."

Tilly laughs. "It'll be fine. You're meeting your family. They are going to be so happy to see you, Hayley."

CHAPTER 24

My sister's words play out in my head as we make our way downstairs. "They are going to be so happy to see you, Hayley." If Nora is anything like her family, they will hate me too. Maybe Nora will convince them I'm not Anna, and Tilly and I will be asked to leave. That thought doesn't make me as happy as it did a couple of days ago. I don't know how I feel about that. I guess getting attached was inevitable. They are my family. They want a relationship with me. They won't abandon me like so many foster families did, right?

Aiden and Nick are sitting at the kitchen island that's covered with trays of breakfast foods. Aiden's wearing black slacks and a button-down shirt the same color as my dress. His hair is gelled in the plastic way I'm sure Nora likes. He looks handsome. Nick is wearing gray jeans with a darker gray shirt, a light gray tie, and a black vest. He looks delicious. Dressed up but with style.

Nick basically eye-fucks me. He silently mouths, "Fucking sexy."

I grin and mouth, "Same" to him. He glances down at my feet and chuckles lightly. I narrow my eyes in confusion.

"You look great, Hayley," Aiden says. "And so do you, Tilly."

Nick pulls out the chair between him and Aiden. "Better eat up so you can stomach today, princess."

"Stop. It's not going to be that bad," Aiden says with a smile. "You're going to make her fake being sick or some shit."

I laugh as I sit down because that is my plan. Tilly takes the seat next to Aiden and grabs a chocolate chip muffin.

"No shoes?" Nick whispers in my ear as his hand settles on my thigh over my dress.

"I'm inside. Why would I need shoes?" I look down at his feet to see he's wearing black sneakers. Aiden has on loafers, and Tilly has on white flats. I'm the only one without shoes.

Nick grips my dress, inching it up until he can slip his hand under. His fingers instantly find my sex, and I raise a brow. He smiles and rubs his fingers back and forth over my silk panties. I lean my chest against the island edge to hide Nick's hand.

"Sleep okay?" Aiden asks.

I nod, afraid to use my words because Nick has pushed my panties aside and is circling my clit. As good as it feels, I grab his wrist and pull his hand away. He sips his coffee while I straighten my dress. "Not here," I whisper. "Bathroom in five?"

Nick grins. "Hell ya."

"Morning," Rocco says, sauntering into the kitchen wearing gray slacks and a black button-down shirt. He takes the seat next to Tilly and grabs a muffin.

"Are you nervous?" Aiden asks me.

"No. Not really."

"Hayley is rarely ever nervous. Mom used to joke she wasn't born with the fear gene," Tilly says.

"I'm full." Nick stretches and then stands. "Going to make a couple calls before the party starts. See you guys in a bit."

He traces a finger over my back on his way out of the kitchen and Tilly notices. She smiles and raises a brow. I stick my tongue out at her and she laughs.

"What's so funny?" Aiden asks.

"Nothing," I say. "My sister is goofy. Are you excited to see your family?"

"I saw them a couple months ago during spring break, but it's always nice to spend time with them." He rubs the back of his neck. "I should warn you. Mom is a mess right now. There's still tension between her and her family."

"Why?"

"Mom thinks they're still mad she ran off with Dad. She was engaged to someone else at the time. A family friend."

I reach across the counter and grab a donut. "Do

they not like John?"

"They... to be honest, they're a little hard on him. They were mad about the marriage and then you were kidnapped. He wasn't home when it happened. Mom was here with you, me, Nick, and Colt. Mom had postpartum from Colt. Our grandmother was angry Dad wasn't here to help her with so many kids, but he was only gone for a few hours. He couldn't be home every second."

"Nick was here?"

"Yeah. Mom was watching him while his parents were on a business trip. I wanted you to know the history, so if you noticed any tension, you'd know it's not your fault."

"Thanks for the heads up... shit, what do I call these people? Are they going to expect me to call them Grandma and Grandpa? Aunt and Uncle?"

"Oh, I... I don't know. I call our grandparents Mormor and Morfar, but Colt calls them Gran and Grandad. I guess do what makes you feel comfortable. Mom has five sisters and three brothers. We have a dozen cousins, but I don't think all of them are coming. They didn't want to overwhelm you. Oh, and Nick's parents will be here, but they're coming later this evening."

My eyes widen, and I set down the half-eaten donut. "Shit. I have to... shit. Excuse me." I hurry from the kitchen and race to the closest bathroom. It's empty. Maybe we should have agreed on a specific bathroom. I move to another bathroom and swing the door open. I smile. "You're still here."

Nick grabs me around the waist and pulls me against him, kicking the door closed. "Of course I'm still here. I'd wait all day. Have you seen the way you look? My dick sprung to life when you walked into the kitchen."

Staring into his dark chocolate-colored eyes, I laugh as he brings the straps down on my dress. It falls to my feet, leaving me in white satin panties. I rub my hand over the bulge in Nick's pants before undoing the button and zipping them down. His black boxer briefs are tight around his thick thighs. He kicks his pants to the corner of the bathroom and lifts me up onto the white vanity countertop, putting my hips perfectly in line with his.

I want to undress him completely, but we don't have time for that. I pull him free from his boxers and stroke his shaft as he kisses along my neck and shoulders. His fingers slip into my panties. God, I'm wet. His fingers glide through my folds and then slip right into my core with ease. His two fingers work me while my hand works him. His mouth finds mine, but the kiss ends too soon.

I look up at him with hooded eyes wondering why he stopped kissing me. His heated gaze is on my center watching his fingers move in and out. I want to drop my head to my shoulders and close my eyes, but I like to watch him watch.

"These pretty little panties are in the way of my pretty pussy." The sound of fabric fills the room as

Nick rips them from my body.

I laugh lightly as I stare at the white silk in his hands.

I brace myself with my hands on the counter behind me as he takes in my naked body.

"Fuck, so beautiful." He strokes his dick as he lines himself up with my center. I scoot forward to get the angle right as he guides himself into me. Both of his hands come to either side of my ass, and he grips me there hard. I love it.

Our mouths collide while he begins to pump into me. I'm a little sore from yesterday, but my body adjusts quickly, my pussy getting wetter. A few moans escape, but I'm trying to keep them in. My boobs bounce as he begins to pump faster. He dips his head to bite and lick. I throw my head back and arch my back to give him better access to my chest. Holy shit, this is heaven.

His arms move under my thighs and his hands grip my hips as he tugs me forward. I keep my hands braced behind myself as my ass leaves the counter completely. He kisses me roughly as he plows into my wet heat. I want to touch my clit. I'm so close to an orgasm.

He pulls away from my mouth to fuck me hard for a few minutes, my tits bouncing so much they hurt. My crown's slipping, but I don't give a fuck.

"Fuck," Nick grunts. "Feels so damn good." He sets me back on the counter and moves his fingers to my clit as he continues to pump into me.

The crown falls from my head and clatters

against the counter. Nick circles my clit and then pinches. I come so fucking hard. I squeeze my eyes shut and hold my breath as my muscles contract. He stops moving completely while I ride it out.

Once I come back down, I take in a lung full of air, and he grabs my ass with both of his hands and begins to move. The sound of our skin slapping together fills the bathroom. He says something and then he's pulling out and spilling himself over my pussy. He dips his head and bites my left tit and then sucks my nipple into his mouth as he continues pumping himself with his hand.

We're both breathing hard and covered in sweat. That was hot. I've never been fucked on a counter before.

Nick drops a kiss to my shoulder. "Damn, you have some good pussy, so fucking tight."

I laugh. "Only because you're so big."

He grunts and grabs a cloth from the drawer next to my leg. He's gentle and thorough as he cleans me up, and then helps me back into my dress.

"Fuck. My dick's hard again." He buries his face into my neck and kisses me there. "I can't get enough of you."

The feeling is mutual. I'm ready for round two, but unfortunately, there isn't time. I have to meet a bunch of royals.

***

Claire was right about the hair, it stayed in place

even though the crown didn't. I place it on my head and then head back to the kitchen while Nick heads the other way saying he'll meet me there in a minute. Aiden, Rocco, and Tilly are still eating breakfast when I walk in, and Nora's pacing the kitchen with a phone clutched to her ear.

She angrily drops the phone to the kitchen counter and spins around with wild eyes. "Martin forgot to get the crab claws." She begins to babble in another language as she hurries from the room and it hits me.

"Does your family speak English?" I ask Aiden.

"Our family," Aiden corrects. "And, yeah, they all speak English, some better than Americans. Their main language is Swedish but they all know multiple languages and most of our cousins, aunts, and uncles went to American boarding schools."

"As long as they speak English."

"Don't lie," Tilly says. "You would have preferred it if there was a language barrier."

"Shh, you little savage." I chew my lip. "Boarding school. That's what the art school is, huh?"

"It is. A top-rated one," Aiden says. "I looked it up online."

Tilly beams and my stomach turns. She jumps headfirst into things without thinking them through. She'll be with mega-rich snobby assholes. I don't want to see her lose herself. "You better message me every day and call every weekend or I'm flying over there," I tell her, and I mean it.

"I will, and Nora spoke with the school. I can take time off to visit Dad when he's ready."

"Good. He'll want to see you. You're his favorite."

"Am not. He always favored you," Tilly says.

"Shut up. You're everyone's favorite," I say as Nora rushes back into the room. She's in one of her red-carpet gowns. It's golden, shiny, and leaves her slim shoulders bare. It's more form-fitting than her usual dresses. Nora's hips are narrow and so is her waist. I don't think I've seen her eat. Maybe she's on a water diet. Or maybe she feeds off souls.

"They will be here any second." She claps her hands together loudly. "Move to the front porch to greet everyone properly." She glances at me and then stiffens. "Your piercings," she hisses.

"I think they go with my dress." I hold in a smirk. "Do you like the crown?" I say, making sure she sees it.

"It's fine, Mom. Nobody will even notice," Aiden says, trying to appease the psychopath.

"It's not fine, but I don't have time for this." She flicks her wrist. "Hurry to the front."

Nick finds me as we're all walking past the library. "I couldn't stand to be in the kitchen with you. I would have bent you over the kitchen counter. Your warm skin tone goes so well with the marble," he whispers near my ear.

I elbow him in the ribs because Tilly's next to me and turns bright red. Thankfully everyone else doesn't seem to be paying attention.

Nick chuckles and catches up to walk beside Aiden. I pluck the crown from my head and set it next to a vase of flowers in the hall as we're passing it.

"So, you and Nick," Tilly says, eyeing me with a smug expression.

All I can do is laugh.

"You two look good together, really good. And you look happy when you're near him."

I bite my lip. I could see myself with Nick which means I need to talk to him before feelings start to develop. I can rein them in if this is casual. I could fuck around with him a few more times. The sex is definitely worth it.

"What are you thinking about?" Tilly says, grinning. "You look happy."

"Chocolate cake," I tell her as we step out onto the concrete porch.

She giggles. "You must really like chocolate cake."

I chuckle. "It's not code for anything, Tilly, geez."

"Anna, come to the front. You should be the first person everyone sees." Nora pulls me away from my smiling sister to stand near the steps.

She arranges Aiden a step behind me, Rocco and Nick behind him, and Tilly in the back. Nora moves down the steps to look at us. She frowns but several limos pull up as she's opening her mouth. The color drains from her face, and she hurries up the steps to stand next to Aiden.

256

"Everyone smile," she snaps.

I glance over my shoulder to see Tilly standing alone in the back, twirling her hair and chewing her lip. "Psst." I jut my chin. "Come here," I hiss.

She does, and I take her hand, holding her close beside me. Everyone seems to be holding their breath as the limos' engines shut off.

CHAPTER 25

One moment it's completely quiet, and the next, it's chaotic. It reminds me of an antique sale Nana had at her church last month and forced Tilly and me to go. There were hundreds of old people dressed in their Sunday best running toward the church doors when they opened.

Only now, the people are rushing toward me. I didn't expect everyone to swarm me like they do. I don't know why I didn't expect it. They all talk at once, their voices drowning each other out. Someone laughs, and then another. The colors of their clothes blur together. A high pitch squeal causes my ears to ring. I turn my head when my hair is tugged, putting me face to face with a man who's speaking quickly in another language. My chest tightens and I squeeze my eyes shut before taking a deep breath. I back up to give myself some space, but I bump into a woman, almost knocking her down.

I can't move. Harsh chemicals assault my nose. I don't understand why people wear perfume. I hate it. This is too fucking much. My legs are shaking, and I know I'm about to collapse. These people will trample me to death. I need to stay up. I need to run. I ball my hands into fists.

"Move!"

The harsh voice isn't mine, but it's exactly what I wanted to say. The crowd doesn't move, if anything, they close in further.

"Stop crowding her! Get back!"

Someone grabs my arm and tugs. Elbows and arms knock into me as I move through the circle of people until I'm on the other side. Tilly. My sister is the one who pulled me out.

"You okay?"

I step farther from the circle. Only a couple of people seem to notice I'm not where I was a second ago. They are all still talking and laughing. I can't make out anything being said. It's rattling my brain.

"Why don't we move inside!" Nora hollers, ushering everyone toward the door. She begins talking over everyone in a language sounding similar to French.

"Hayley." Nick's hand brushes against my lower back. "Are you okay?"

"This is insane," I say, still trying to calm down. Those people are extremely lucky I didn't start swinging. I was so close.

"Can you make sure they don't crowd her again?

She can't handle—"

"It's fine, Tilly. I lost my head for a second. I'll tell them to back off if it happens again."

We're at the back of the slow-moving crowd. I don't think anyone has noticed where I went. I don't see Aiden or Rocco. They must be at the front of the mob which has already made it inside.

"Where's Casey?" I ask Nick.

"With some chick. Nora didn't want him here for this. She doesn't really like Casey."

"Oh, there are people she likes? Could have fooled me."

Nick chuckles.

Up ahead, I hear Nora's strained voice, but the crowd is mostly talking over her.

"Let me see what's going on or we'll be out here all day," Nick says, moving past me to squeeze through to the front.

I feel the air conditioning blowing against my sticky skin. Finally, the crowd starts to move faster, and we make it inside, closing the doors behind us. Keeping distance, Tilly and I follow the crowd down the hall. I hold my stomach and groan. "I think breakfast isn't sitting right with me."

Tilly laughs. "Shut up. You didn't even eat breakfast."

We walk into the large formal room where tables of food and drinks have been lined against the wall. The multiple couches that are normally in this room are gone and have been replaced with six round tables covered with white cloth. Each table has five chairs covered with blue cloth and held together with a white bow. Even with the tables in the room, there is still plenty of space.

Tilly gestures for me to follow her to where Aiden, Nick, and Rocco are standing next to the table closest to us. I like my spot by the door, but I see some people eyeing me, so I follow Tilly.

"Graysen's here," I hear Aiden say as we approach.

"No shit? Why did Nora invite him?" Nick hisses.

I want to ask them who they're talking about but a really old lady with a saggy face steps into my path. Her teeth are yellow and her smile wide. She latches on to my arm with her bony hand.

"Hi, who are you?" Tilly asks the old lady.

The old lady mumbles something, pats my cheek, and then hobbles away on a cane. "She was like a hundred years old. I hope I don't live that long."

Tilly laughs and drags me the last couple of feet to the table. The guys stop talking, and Aiden settles his arm over my shoulders.

"You okay?" Aiden asks.

"This way, Anna! Aiden, bring her over here." Nora's voice booms over the chatter of the crowd. "Up to the front! You can come over here."

"I'll stay with you," Aiden says. "It won't be so bad once everyone calms down."

He ushers me forward, but I look over my shoulder at Tilly.

"Go. I'll be fine. Rocco and I are going to hit up the food. I think I saw cupcakes."

"I know you'll be fine," I say. "I won't. Come with me."

Tilly laughs and shakes her head. "This is too much for even me. Good luck." She gives me a thumbs-up and then drags Rocco toward the tables.

That side of the room is free of people. Lucky bitch. Aiden takes my right and Nick my left as we make our way to the front of the room. People try to reach out and touch me as I pass by, but Nick shields me with his body.

On the other side of the crowd, Nora is standing next to the stone fireplace. She holds out her hand for me to take, but fuck that. When she decided to send my sister away without talking to me is when I decided to cut her out. She is not my mother, and I'm not going to play nice. I ignore her hand and instead stand on her right side a few feet away. Aiden takes my left and Nick stands next to him.

"You're so beautiful, Anna!"

"Look how pretty she is."

"Look how alike they look."

The crowd is oohing and aahing, some in English and some in another language, while Nora hushes everyone.

"Unfortunately, Anna only speaks English. Like I said in the email, she's had a rough time and will probably need to rest soon. Be patient with her."

What the fuck is Nora talking about? She's acting like she cares, but I know she doesn't. Whatever, I like the part where I'll need to rest soon.

The crowd starts to move in but Nick steps in front of me. "Not everyone at once."

"Why doesn't everyone take a seat and Anna can come by each table?" Nora suggests.

I hate that idea, but I hate standing up here even more. The crowd begins to disperse while Nora helps them find their seats. Over by the door, I notice two guys and a girl. They stand out because they look my age while everyone else looks old as shit. Our family doesn't age well.

"Everyone will calm down in a minute. They're just excited," Aiden says.

"It's fine," I say, throwing him a quick smile and then my gaze is back on the three by the door. The girl has long dark blonde hair. She's wearing a dark blue dress with a plunging V and slits up the sides that reach her thighs. She seems bored as she scrolls through her phone.

My gaze drifts to the blond boy who's staring at me with intensity. He's dressed in a black suit and gray tie. His hair is blond, wavy, and the length is right below his ears.

The guy next to him is wearing blue jeans with a gray shirt and black suit jacket. His brown hair is shaved into a buzz cut. My gaze moves back to the attractive blond. He's still staring at me. His lips tip up into a smirk, and I smile back, and then frown and look away.

Shit.

I probably just checked out my cousin. I get a free pass because I forgot I'm related to everyone in the room. Wow. That is perspective. My genetics come from these people.

"You are beautiful, darling."

A gentle hand lands on my bare upper arm. The woman before me looks to be in her seventies. Her hair is gray and short. Her eyes. "We have the same eyes," I say.

She grins. "Aiden too. I feel so special my twin grandchildren have my eyes."

"You're my grandmother?"

"I am, and I'm so happy to see you again." Her warm hand cups my cheek. "The last time I saw you, you had snuck a piece of strawberry cake and were eating it under the dining room table." She laughs, her hand dropping away. "You were... what is the American word? Headstrong?" She laughs again. "Just like me." She studies my piercings and hair. "A strong princess you've become." She moves her focus to the guys. "Aiden, you're looking as handsome as ever," she says with a smile. "And, Dominick, it's good to see you. We missed you for spring break."

Aiden kisses the woman's cheek, and then says something in what I'm assuming is Swedish.

She laughs and says something in her native language, and then takes my hand. "I look forward to getting to know you." Her gaze drifts to Nora who is staring at us with narrowed eyes. "My daughter is impatient." She winks. "I'll let the others have their time with you, and I'll see you soon."

"Okay," I say a little breathlessly because I didn't expect to like anyone here. My grandmother is cool. Her accent is thick, but it wasn't hard to understand her.

Nora waves me over with that tight smile on her face. I roll my eyes but walk over to her and let her lead me to a table near the food. The only open chair is between two women wearing big floppy hats. Aiden and Nick hover while I mostly listen to the guests at the table speak. A few throw out questions I or Aiden answer. I find out the women wearing the hats are Nora's aunts and the men beside them are their husbands.

I'm starting to relax when Nora ushers us to the next table full of my aunts and uncles. They are lively and excited. I find myself smiling without being forced. It's kind of cool to meet all these people. My family.

Nora ushers me to a table filled with my cousins. Two of my cousins, Molly and Aron are my age, but the others are several years older. I recognize Molly as the girl who was standing at the door with the two guys.

Table after table asks the same questions and compares Aiden and me. There are a lot of pictures, smiles, and hugs. I'm exhausted.

"Excuse us. Princess Anna will be back." Nick wraps his arms around my waist. "You look like you could use a break," he whispers near my ear.

Nick has perfect timing because I was nodding off. He guides me over to a drink table and hands me a glass filled with something pink and bubbly.

"Thank you. If only this was a beer." I throw back half of it.

He scans the room. "What do you think so far?"

I finish the drink and set the glass down. "It's going better than I thought it would. My grandmother is cool, Aunt Alice is a talker, and my cousin Leo, who is twice my age, was totally checking me out, but everyone seems nice so far."

"Watch out for your Uncle William; he likes to talk extensively about the family line. He can go on for hours and hours." Nick points to a man in tweed over by a table filled with different kinds of meats. "And he's on the verge of going deaf, so he yells everything."

I laugh. "Thanks for the heads up." My gaze slowly wanders the room. There she is. Tilly and Rocco are at a table with my grandmother, and another woman that looks familiar, but all the faces are blurring together.

"Nick, over here. I need your help," Nora calls from the doorway.

Nick lays his hand on my waist, squeezing gently. "I'll be back." He presses his lips to my temple, and my eyes dart around to see if anyone noticed. "Maybe I can steal you away soon."

"Yes, please," I whisper, biting my lip and growing warm. I watch him walk away. Dammit, that boy is gorgeous. I can't wait to undress him later.

"Hello, Princess Anna."

"Hi," I say to the cousin I was checking out earlier. He's even cuter up close. His eyes are bright blue and seem to shine as he takes me in. The stubble along his jaw is a shade darker than his wavy blond hair.

"I'm Graysen. Our parents grew up together."

His accent is thick, but it's not the same as everyone else's. "Grew up together? So, we aren't cousins?"

He grins, showing off dimples that add to his attractive "boy next door" look. "No. I wouldn't have been checking out my cousin for the last hour." He glances over his shoulder as the guy he was standing next to earlier approaches. "This is Colin Davies. He isn't your cousin either. We live in England."

"Noted, family friends."

"Graysen. I saw you and your father are here. I didn't know either of you were invited," Nick says, wrapping his arm around my waist and pulling me to his side.

My brows pull together at Nick's public display and cold tone.

Graysen stares as Nick's fingers skim up and down my arm. "Of course we were invited. Nora called us herself," Graysen says, his smile turning stiff.

"And you brought a date?" Nick gestures to Colin.

Graysen chuckles. "My mate from University. This is Colin Davies. He's going to take over his father's million-dollar brewing company."

"That's nice. Excuse us."

I almost get whiplash with how fast Nick spins around and pulls me in the other direction. "Whoa, Nick, what's up?"

"Graysen's an ass."

"How do you know him?"

"Before Nora met John, she was engaged to Alexander, Graysen's dad."

"Why would Nora invite her ex's kid?" I glance over my shoulder to where Graysen is standing and staring at me with narrowed eyes.

"Nick Cabot. Looking as handsome as ever," my cousin says, stepping into our path.

I can't remember her name. Was it Bonnie or Lolly? Whatever her name is, she's staring at Nick like she wants to lick him. She has that wholesome, natural beauty thing going on with her dark blonde hair, blue eyes, pale skin, and rosy cheeks, but there's something about the way her eyes are set that makes her look mischievous. I noticed it an hour ago, and I see it now.

Smirking, she says something in another language that sounds like heart sock nut day, and then something that sounds like fort fond day. Whatever it means, Nick's jaw locks.

His hand falls away from my side. "I'll be right back."

I arch a brow as he storms toward her and grabs

her upper arm. She smiles at me as he pulls her away. I watch them leave the room together. He's not mine, so whatever that was is none of my business.

"Don't tell me you have a thing for Dominick Cabot."

"What?" I spin around to face Graysen and Colin.

"He's nothing," Graysen says, with angry narrowed eyes.

"See how fast she spread her legs?" Colin says.

Glaring at me, Graysen says, "I wasn't told anything about you being involved with someone." He scoffs. "And what do you see in Nick? He's a fucking loser. You need to end it with him."

"Are you still going to agree to it?" Colin asks Graysen, looking disgusted. "She disrespected you. She's a fucking whore." His eyes roam over my body. "She might be attractive, but you know what they say about whores."

Their harsh and confusing words sound so elegant coming out of their mouths that they almost don't piss me off. *Where the fuck did Nick go?* I quickly scan the room and see him by the door talking to my cousin. She's standing way too fucking close to him.

"Anna," Nora says, appearing from out of nowhere.

Her eyes are bright and almost too wide like she's on some type of upper, maybe meth. God, I'm ready to ditch this party. Colin gives me a look of loathing and then walks away.

"I've been looking for you." She grins, her smile manic. It reminds me of a hyena. "I see you've met your fiancé. What a beautiful couple you two make."

My stomach clenches with her words. I'm about to ask her what the hell she's talking about when my cousin's squeal fills the room. I watch as she flings her arms around Nick, lifts herself to the tips of her toes, and presses her lips to his. He doesn't pull away. My eyes are wide and heart rapid. He's not pulling away. Is he fucking kissing her back?

Graysen's hand lands on my shoulder, and his lips feather against my ear. "Does your cousin know you've been fucking her boyfriend?"

Note from the author:

Sorry for the cliffhanger! Book two will be out very soon (I hope). I've been working hard on it, but there are more twists and turns than I was expecting. FYI: Book two is a bit darker than I thought it was going to be. I always let the characters tell their story and what a story it's turning out to be!

If you want to read another one of my books while you wait, I recommend, Found by the Rivers. I just love the characters in this book and their story. If you want to get in touch, I'm all over social media, and If you'd like to leave a review, I would appreciate it so very much!

About the author:

Liberty Freer is a book loving, caffeinated insomniac. She likes to bring her memories to life with twisted truths. She was a bit rebellious in her adolescence and still is at heart. When she isn't writing, she's exploring nature with her two boys.

www.ingramcontent.com/pod-product-compliance
Lightning Source LLC
Chambersburg PA
CBHW031707170626
46808CB00005B/1639